THE PURPLE AUTOMOBILE AND THE NEWSPAPER GIRL

THE PURPLE AUTOMOBILE AND THE NEWSPAPER GIRL

Seymour Z. Mann

For Ralph, my friend of long-standing and for all the trials and tribulations, we have shared. As usual, you beat me to the draw so you are novelist #1 + and I am satisfied with the #2 position. Adults who have read the story tell me it made them forget for awhile the terrible events that are reported each day + make life so stressful. So you and Barbara should both read it.

Seymour.
2/22/04

iUniverse, Inc.
New York Lincoln Shanghai

The Purple Automobile And The Newspaper Girl

iUniverse, Inc.

For information address:
iUniverse, Inc.
2021 Pine Lake Road, Suite 100
Lincoln, NE 68512
www.iuniverse.com

ISBN: 0-595-29907-5 (pbk)
ISBN: 0-595-66076-2 (cloth)

Printed in the United States of America

In Memory of My Father—He Would Have Understood

For Joshua and Shoshana—My Main Muses and My First Editors

CONTENTS

▼

Acknowledgments

There are many to whom acknowledgments are due for what in various ways they contributed to the creative processes which ultimately resulted in the story as it appears here. There are hardly sufficient words to thank Herman Taube, a poet and novelist of note, who has since the early days of my retirement endeavors given me friendship, counsel and constant encouragement. I owe much thanks to Susan Shreve, Professor of English at George Mason University, who is a stimulating teacher of writing and who is a well-established author of adult novels and children's stories. She was a mentor helpful to me in numerous ways, more than I think she knows. In retrospect, I'm sure that the high words of praise she gave to the early stories I wrote were more than a bit exaggerated, and that as such they were intended to keep me writing. To say that those words were music to my ears is an understatement about the significance of their impact upon me.

Special words of gratitude go to my Live Poets Society friend and colleague, Jeanne Patrice Butler, who graciously gave of her artistic talents to produce the illustrations that accompany this story. I must also record recognition to Lou Susshotz whose patience with me was never-ending as he used his computer knowledge and skills to resolve the technical problems that arose during the manuscript's preparation.

The dedication page for this story displays my feelings for what my grandchildren have contributed to my writing efforts of these past years. The love they shower upon me gives warmth and meaning to my living. Much encouragement and critical help also came from the children whose classrooms I invaded and who attentively listened as I read for them my stories.

Within just hours of this writing my wife and I will usher in the beginning of our 62nd year of marriage. Her companionship has sustained and supported me beyond measure. It is of good fortune that she serves for me as the most honest and often the most severe critic of my creative efforts; however, her observations and evaluations are always given with a ribbon of love tied around them.

Preface

At this point in my life I feel comfortable in claiming that my major work activity embraces the writing of stories for children and young adults and a commitment to the study and writing of poetry. I did not, however, seriously engage in such until my post-retirement years. It is true that in my pre-retirement career writing was an integral aspect of my professional life. During that almost fifty-year span I did establish a quite respectable publication record. That body of work, though, did not fall under the category of creative writing, nor was it of literary merit as that term is commonly used.

So how come is it that already in the eighth decade of living I am involved in what might appropriately be labeled as a new career? The answer to that question offered here is but a brief recap of the complexity of circumstances and attitudes out of which arose the legitimacy of attaching that label to the slice of life referred to as my senior years. When I decided to retire somewhat earlier than had been my original intentions, friends and colleagues peppered me with questions about what I intended to do in my post-retirement life. Since at that point in time the only thing that I was sure of was that I wanted to make a rather sharp break from the sorts of matters and activities that consumed the bulk of my time and efforts as demanded by my professional obligations. After constantly being pressed to give a more serious and detailed answer to the "what are you are you going to do" questions, I then offered a concrete response that I thought then was more in jest than fact. My answer was, "I'm going to devote my time to writing stories for children." Probably because the questioners thought I was slightly daft or pulling their collective legs, their annoying questions ceased.

Subsequent to our move from New York City to our retirement abode in Virginia, there was an unexpected hiatus when it was not possible for me to engage in any of the activities I thought I might choose to pursue. During that period of imposed inactivity and reflection time, I came to realize that there was more truth than jest to the response about my intentions given to those who posed the queries. It became clear to me that the possibility of returning in a serious way to my long-ago interest in the writing of stories and poetry was lurking in my mind for some time. Memories of how much I loved and enjoyed the creative process especially during my lower school and higher education years pressed with vigor to the forefront of my mind. There also emerged into consciousness another significant item. It was the recall of the pleasure I received from the telling of my invented stories to my children, to nieces and nephews and sundry others who always clamored for their telling and retelling. This usually occurred whenever there was a celebratory or observational event that meant an extended family gathering. I knew, too, that I was always conscious of the ever-present "kidhood" that is so much a part of my persona.

Well, the inchoate possibility lurking in my mind more than a decade and a half ago did become a reality. Whether this late-in-life commitment to a writing life may or may not constitute a new career is really beside the point, and it is not of significance to me. The points of real significance for me are that the writing of stories for children and young people of various ages has nurtured and enriched my imaginative and creative capacities; has put me in intimate touch with the years of my boyhood; has led me to a heightened appreciation of the wealth of experiences from my pre-retirement career that in a mysterious and strange manner are woven into the fabric of my stories; has in many ways made easier the weathering of the trials that inevitably come with advancing age; and it has brought me to new friends and savvy mentors. I must add to this litany of satisfactions the one that I deem of utmost importance—namely, that despite the frustrations that are inherent in the story writing process, it has brought enjoyment and sheer fun of immense proportions to my later years.

I trust that those who read or hear the story presented in the following pages will be swept up in the same feelings of excitement that I experienced in its writing. I would hope, too, that in addition to the pleasure and satisfaction derived from its reading, that from it readers would gain insights about their own ambitions; would gain some enhanced understanding about relationships with peers and the significance of friendships; and would gain an enlarged appreciation about the valuable role adults can and should play in their lives.

Seymour Z. Mann
Alexandria, Virginia
August 28, 2003

CHAPTER 1

▼

THURSDAY AFTERNOON ON A WARM SPRING DAY

Angie Inkster Scrivener sat on the front porch steps of her house. At the moment she was not a happy fifth grader, and she showed it with the pout on her face. She was also talking to herself, and if you were in earshot you would hear her saying not very nice things about her school, her English teacher and some of her classmates. Every once in a while her hand flew up to her head, and she would first tug on a clump of her curly dark hair followed immediately by slapping herself on the forehead. With each slap Angie would mutter, "Dummy, dummy."

Such behavior was quite unusual for Angie. She loved school and she was very much liked by her classmates. She always completed her work on time, she received good marks, and her teachers often praised her. During all of the last week, though, she did not turn in any of her homework assignments, and for the first time in her whole life she flunked a test in her best subject—English.

Though Angie was not aware of it, her mother was at their kitchen window watching all the crazy things Angie was doing to herself. Mrs. Scrivener was very worried about her daughter. She knew something was wrong, but Angie refused to talk about what was bothering her despite the number of times Mrs. Scrivener tried to engage her in a conversation. Now seeing how upset Angie was, her Mom decided that it was time to get to the bottom of her daughter's problem.

AN UPSET AND ANGRY ANGIE SITTING ON THE
STEPS OF THE SCRIVENER'S FRONT PORCH

Angie was so wrapped up in her anger and feeling sorry for herself that she never heard her Mom's footsteps as she came down the stairs to sit on the step next to her. She was startled by her Mom's voice so close to her ear saying in a very firm tone, "Don't move, Angie Inkster Scrivener. We're going to have a talk, and this time there is no escaping it."

"There's nothing to talk about. I'm mad! That's all there is to it."

"Well," said Mrs. Scrivener, "if you're angry it must be about something. All this crazy and unusual behavior of yours tells me that what has caused all this upset is something that is important to you. Now, out with it."

At first Angie didn't respond to her mother, then suddenly tears came to her eyes and she began to sob. Her Mom did not say anything, but she gently hugged her daughter after which Angie buried her head in her Mom's lap. She remained in that position for a few moments as she continued with her soft crying.

Almost as quickly as she started her sobbing it stopped. She sat up, threw her arms around her Mom and, whispered to her, "I do love you, Mom, and I'm sorry for the way I've been acting."

Mrs. Scrivener held her daughter's face between her hands and looked her straight in the eyes as she said, "Listen, pretty girl, I like your dark eyes better without tears pouring from them. I believe your sadness and hurt will go away if you'll give me a clue as to what caused all of this. If we know the problem, we'll probably be able to help you do something about it."

"Okay, Mom," responded Angie as she lifted her face from between her Mom's hands, "I'm going to wash away the smudges on my face. Then we'll sit down and talk."

Angie and her mother sat across from each other at their kitchen table. They were having a serious conversation. Mrs. Scrivener learned from her daughter's story of the things happening in her school and the reason for Angie's peculiar behavior. It was all about a writing contest in her English class to see who would win the honor of being named as the fifth grade's representative on the Plainview School Banner, her school newspaper.

A written essay was required for each person in the class who wanted to be named to that fifth grade reporter's job. The assigned topic for those who chose to compete for the job was, "Why I Would Like To Be A Reporter For The Plainview School Banner." Its length could not be more than 500 words.

When Angie's Mom heard that she said, "Well, I'm sure that wasn't a hard job for you. You always said that with a middle name like Inkster and with your last name being Scrivener, you were born to be a writer."

"I know, Mom. That is what I wrote about, but I started with something else. I hate to say it, but I made another mistake too."

"So what wrong thing did you write about? And what was your second mistake?"

Angie then told her mother what the first reason was that she gave for wanting the fifth grade reporting job: "It was important," she said, "because it would show Benjee something about me. I wanted my brother to know that he isn't the only writer in the family."

"I gather your English teacher didn't think very much of that reason. What sort of comments did he make that explained his objections to that idea?"

"Well, Mr. Story said that a lot of things in my essay except that part were good, but it was inappropriate to write, 'I want to be the fifth grade reporter because I'm jealous of my brother in the eighth grade who is the editor of the Banner.' Even though I insisted the sentence belonged in the essay because it was true, Mr. Story repeated his objection to it."

Hearing that Mrs. Scrivener couldn't suppress a grin as she told Angie, "I guess that wasn't very appropriate, but I've warned you that being jealous of Benjee all the time was not a good idea. But you must have written more than that in a 500 word essay."

"I did write more, Mom, a lot more. Here, I'll read you a part of it." Angie then pulled some folded-up sheets of paper from the pocket of her jeans and after smoothing them out read aloud this section of her essay:

> I am very proud of my name, even if Inkster seems like a funny name for a girl. My mother chose it as my middle name because it was her last name before she was married, and she often told me it was an important name that should always be remembered. Once a long time ago one of her ancestors became known as Mr. Inkster because he always came home from work with ink stains on his hands and face. He was a famous printer and typesetter who made books from other people's handwriting. From that time on becoming a printer was a tradition for some members of the family in each generation—as my Uncle Joe is today.
>
> My last name is from my Dad's family, and Scrivener means writer or scribe. As my father explained it to me many times, the story in his family was that far back in Jewish history some of his ancestors were scribes who copied the words from the Holy Books to the parchment sections of the Torah scrolls. Some were also teachers of those books, and they wrote many things about them. From that time on until today there were family members on my Dad's side who were Rabbis, some who became well-known authors and others, like my Dad, who became teachers.
>
> So with the name Angie Inkster Scrivener I always knew I wanted to be a writer. When I was a third grader I made up my mind that when I grew up I would be a reporter on a big city newspaper and then probably a famous television interviewer, like Barbara Walters, Diane Sawyer, or Katie Couric.

When she finished reading the last sentence of that part of her essay Angie tore up the pages, crumpled the pieces into a ball and tossed them into the nearby waste basket as she spat out the words, "So much for that!"

"Calm down, and don't get in a tiff again," Mrs. Scrivener reminded Angie. "Now tell me, didn't your teacher think that part you just read to me was quite interesting and nice enough to overcome the inappropriate thing you wrote about at the beginning?"

"Mr. Story liked that part a lot, but, Mom, I did the dumbest, stupidest thing. I forgot to pay attention to the rules, and I just kept writing and writing. The print-out from our computer was almost five pages long."

"So Mr. Story didn't accept your essay for the contest because its length was at least 1500 words instead of keeping it to 500?"

"That's right, Mom, and my stupid brother is really teasing me about it. And the worst thing is that the essay chosen as the winner was Nancy's—my best friend! Now I'll have to hate her because she'll be teasing me about my big, dumb mistakes. The worst part is that she will get to be a reporter, and I never will. What am I going to do, Mom?"

"I guess teasing from your brother was to be expected, but 'hate' is a pretty strong word to use about your best friend. You know, you're no Miss Innocent. I've heard you teasing Nancy about one thing or another plenty of times. Now, if you'll promise to stop being miserable and goofing off at school, it so happens that I know a way for you to get back on track about becoming a reporter."

On hearing those words from her mother, Angie immediately perked up and became very excited, "I promise, I promise. How, Mom? Tell me, tell me, quick, tell me." And with that she jumped up, dashed around the table, and gave her a big kiss.

Actually, Mrs. Scrivener didn't tell Angie anything specific about how to get back on track to being a reporter. Instead, she gave Angie a copy of that day's morning newspaper. The Herald was the paper published in the big city that was near their town of Plainview. When her Mom gave her the paper she told Angie, "Take it to your room and carefully study it. If you are as good a reader as I think you are, I'm sure you'll find that other chance at getting to be a reporter."

Once in her room Angie spread the morning paper on the floor, kneeled down over it and began turning each page looking at each news story to see if she could find what her mother said was there. Finally, in the section of the paper that carried community news items she spotted a story about the paper expanding its coverage of happenings in the town of Plainview. And there it was—the announcement of a competition to select a Junior Reporter. This is what Angie saw:

Morning Herald Soon To Select A Plainview Junior Reporter

We announce today a competition to select a Plainview Junior Reporter. The young person selected will have the opportunity to regularly file interesting news stories from his or her community. The competition will be open to boys and girls who are in the 5th, 6th, 7th or 8th grades of a Plainview school. If you wish to enter please complete the form printed below and attach it to a story covering some event or happening in your community that you believe is newsworthy and will be of interest to our readers. All entries should be in newspaper story style, and the deadline for entries to be received at the **Herald** main office is ten days from today.

Angie read the story over three times: the first time was a silent reading; the second time she read it aloud, but in a quiet voice; and at the third reading she was practically shouting. She was very excited. Then she jumped up, grabbed a scissors from her desk and carefully clipped out the competition entry form. She held it up to kiss it. Then she spoke in a very firm and determined voice several times as if she were making a promise to herself, **"I am going to be the Plainview Junior Reporter!"**

As she tacked the entry form on the bulletin board above her desk, several thoughts were on her mind: *Now I have to find some Plainview happening or event that will be a good subject for a news story. What if my editor brother decides he is going to try for the Junior Reporter's job and I have to compete against him? I absolutely must be the winner because that'll show Nancy just who is the best reporter in our class.*

Just as these and other similar sorts of thoughts were popping into her head, Angie heard her mother call, "Angie Inkster Scrivener, have you forgotten about dinner and your responsibility for setting the table?"

I'll be right there, Mom," she shouted through her closed door, "I guess I lost track of the time."

Though Angie could hardly contain her excitement, she quietly did her job of setting the dining room table. When the task was done she called to her Mom who was still in the kitchen finishing her preparations for the evening meal, "I'm going to check out the early evening news on TV. Call me if you need me, Ma."

Mrs. Scrivener knew immediately that something was up because Angie going to watch TV at that time was different from their usual evening ritual. Normally, when her table setting was finished she came into the kitchen for conversation with her mother. It was then that Angie usually reviewed her day with her mother and told her about the good things that happened in school. At least that was the regular routine when Angie was not in one of her black moods, as she was during the past week. Mrs. Scrivener thought about the situation for a moment or two and then said to herself,

I'm sure she found the newspaper article about the Junior Reporter competition. I guess her ignoring our together time in order to watch the news must have something to do with what she read in the HERALD.

Of course, Mrs. Scrivener was correct in her thinking. What Angie was hoping to see was a report about some Plainview local happening that might give her an idea for the sort of story she could write to submit as her Junior Reporter competition entry.

So Angie carefully watched and listened to all the television news reports. There were reports about the day's events in Congress; she watched a part of the President's news conference; she gave close attention to the weather forecast; she gave half an ear to the local area traffic conditions and to the news about all the robberies and the other bad things that occurred during the preceding night.

As the early evening news report was coming to a close she was quite disappointed that no idea came to her for a story as a result of what she saw and heard on the program. She started to punch the remote to turn off the TV when she heard the anchorwoman say, "Folks, here is one last local item. A person who said he was a resident in the neighboring community of Plainview dropped off at the station what he said was a home video shot of a mystery car that appeared on their main business street about sunrise this morning. Here it is, but pay close attention because it is a very short clip that takes only a few seconds."

What flashed on the screen then was the craziest looking automobile Angie ever saw. It was streaking down Blossom Avenue, Plainview's main street, and it was painted the most dazzling purple one could imagine. Angie saw that it did have four wheels like an ordinary automobile, but its shape was very peculiar. She got only a brief glimpse of it, but to her it seemed to look more like the sleek racing boats she sometimes saw speeding on the big lake at the edge of town where Blossom Avenue ended.

The TV screen went blank as the video clip ended. Then it came alive with the anchorperson expressing amazement at the funny looking car and saying, "The only other item we can report about the purple mystery car at this time is one piece of information phoned to us by a man who claimed he took the shot you just saw. He told our telephone receptionist that there were absolutely no windows on the vehicle. The caller also mentioned that there was a bubble-like dome on the car's top with something he thought he saw in it that was going around and around like a spinning top. If anyone else in Plainview sees the peculiar shaped purple automobile, please give us a call and try to take a picture of it. Good evening. See you on our late news show."

Now Angie shut off the TV, did some cartwheels across the room, and then walked on her hands back to the couch while she said to herself, *Yes, yes, I've got it. That's my story for the competition. I'm going to find that car and its owner, and then I'll be the first reporter to get to the bottom of the mystery of the purple automobile. But no one is going to know about my investigation until I've found the answers, written the story and delivered it to the HERALD. And that goes especially for my snippety, dorky brother.*

After her gymnastics and all the to-herself talking, Angie sat on the couch for a few moments to catch her breath and bring her excitement under control. Then she marched into the kitchen to see if her Mom could use some further help.

"Hi there, young lady," was Mrs. Scrivener's greeting as Angie pushed open the kitchen's swinging door, "I gather there's something up your sleeve about the HERALD's Junior Reporter competition."

"C'mon Mom, that wasn't hard to figure out. You're the one who gave me the hint that there was something in today's newspaper I ought to see. I hope you didn't tell Benjee about it too. Did'ya, Mom, did'ya?"

"No, I did not. I haven't seen Benjee since this morning, but he should be home any minute. Your father was going to pick him up at school on his way home."

"Promise me on your mother's honor that you won't tell the stinker anything about it, especially about my entering the competition."

"Why Angie Inkster Scrivener, you know I don't talk to stinkers, and I am sure there are none in this house. To whom could you possibly be referring?"

"That's very cool, Mom. You know I mean Benjee. Now promise! I don't want him or Dad to know. It's a secret just between you and me until the HERALD prints the winning story—and I'm sure it will be mine because I have a lead on a great news item."

"Okay, I promise, I promise. But if it's going to be a secret between us, how about telling me something of the story you have in mind."

"No ma'am, only I know that, and it is going to stay that way until my investigative report is published. That is it, period."

At that moment Benjee and his Dad pounded up the steps of the front porch and into the house. As soon as he was through the front door Angie heard her brother shouting, "Where's my bratty little sister? I've got something she's gonna love to see."

She didn't respond to Benjee's remark, but Angie heard him running from room to room and up and down the stairs looking for her. Finally, he bounded into the kitchen waving a newspaper. Angie thought it was a copy of the HERALD, and she felt her heart beginning to beat very fast. She was sure Benjee was going to tell her that he was entering the competition. But she saw enough of the page he was waving in front of her to realize that it was not the HERALD but a copy of the PLAINVIEW SCHOOL BANNER. That knowledge relieved her fear, and the funny sensation in her chest immediately disappeared.

"Here it is, little sister, hot off the press. It's the first edition under the editorship of yours truly. And look, your friend Nancy has her first story as the fifth grade reporter right on the first page." And then he shoved the paper into Angie's hands.

Benjee thought that news would really get under his sister's skin. Had he delivered such a message an hour earlier, Angie would have been very upset to hear about it. By now, though, she was certain in her own mind that she was going to be the HERALD's Junior Reporter. That made it possible for her to give a very cool response to her brother's taunt: "Nancy's getting published in just a dumb school newspaper doesn't bother me at all. I'm sure she wrote a very nice story, but if you don't mind I'll look at it later. If you'll excuse me, I'm leaving so I can greet my Dad and give him a big hug."

As Angie stalked out of the room, she tossed the BANNER in her brother's direction. Benjee caught it, but his mouth and eyes opened wide as he gawked at his sister leaving the kitchen. Mrs. Scrivener had observed the scene between her daughter and son without saying a word. Now she spoke to Benjee: "Why the silent stare, Benjamin Scrivener? Did she surprise you?"

"Yeah, Mom. Is she sick or something? I thought I would get a big rise out of her with the news about her friend getting a story into our paper."

"Well, maybe she's grown up a bit and is finally learning to ignore your constant teasing. Here, carry this salad bowl into the dining room and put it on the table, and then get yourself cleaned up for dinner. I'll get Angie and your father."

CHAPTER 2

▼

THURSDAY NIGHT

Dinner that night at the Scrivener household was unusually calm and quiet. Every one attentively listened to Mr. Scrivener tell about the new computer network that was being installed in the high school where he taught. He told them that he was pleased and proud that he was given the responsibility for training all the teachers about how to use the network. Neither of her parents needed to remind Angie not to interrupt when someone else was talking. It was the first time in Benjee's memory that she didn't babble about something for the whole meal. He was scheduled to play in an early evening basketball game at the community center, and he was anxious to get up to his room. He knew his parents would insist that he do his homework before he left for the game.

It turned out that everyone in the family except Angie needed to be away from the house for one reason or another during a part of that evening. That suited Angie fine. A plan was forming in her head about investigating the mystery of the purple automobile, and it required some advance preparation that she didn't want anyone else in the family to observe. Finally, the after-dinner clearing of the table and other chores were done, Benjee finished his homework and left for the game, and her Mom and Dad went off to their separate meetings. It was only the second time Angie was allowed to remain in the house by herself at night, and this time she wasn't at all frightened about it.

As soon as she heard the family car leave the driveway she scurried into the kitchen to find the big metropolitan telephone directory that was kept on a pantry shelf. Angie lugged it over to the counter underneath the wall phone, and began rummaging through the pages. She was searching for the telephone number of the TV station. She finally found it listed under the C's. Quickly she punched in the number for Channel 5, KJIH.

When the station receptionist answered, Angie asked, "May I please be connected with someone in the newsroom?" The Channel 5 telephone person rang an extension, and Angie heard a voice announcing, "This is the news editor. Do you have a story or a tip for us?"

Of course, Angie had to say she did not, but she indicated that she would like to ask a question about a story that was on their earlier evening news. Acting like she thought a good reporter would, Angie did not wait for a yes or no answer. Instead, she immediately popped her question, "Since you broadcast the story about the purple mystery auto, has anyone else in Plainview reported seeing it?"

When she heard the news editor say, "No, we have not, but is there something you know about that funny looking purple painted auto you can tell us?" Instantly Angie cut off the conversation by putting the phone back on its hanging cradle so the connection was broken.

The next piece of her plan was to check if the Plainview Police were investigating the case of the mystery car. Angie knew she could reach the police by using the 911 emergency number, but she realized it was not a good idea to do it that way since she really had no emergency to report. Instead, she ruffled through the pages of the phone book again until she found a listing for government offices, and there she found a regular number for Plainview Police Headquarters. She called that number and when the phone was answered she heard: "Plainview Police, Desk Sergeant Jonas on duty here."

At first Angie hesitated about going on with the next step in her plan, but after a second or so she did: "Sergeant Jonas, My name is Sarah Sly and I need some information. You see, I'm doing a report for school on how the police investigate unsolved mysteries. Could you tell me a little bit about how our police department is investigating the mystery of the purple automobile, or whatever sort of vehicle it was, that was seen speeding up Blossom Avenue this morning?"

The thought that right away ran through Angie's mind when the question to the sergeant came out of her mouth was: *Excuse me Mom and Dad, I sort of just told a lie—but I think its okay for a reporter to make up stories to get a story—I hope.* As a matter of fact, she did learn some items of importance from the Plainview Police Desk Sergeant.

He was very patient in explaining that the police in most instances do not give out information about an ongoing investigation unless they believe it will help their investigation. "So, Ms. Sly," she heard him say, "I can only tell you a few things about what stage the case is now at, but I can't give you the full details about what the detectives on this case are actually doing to solve the mystery."

Angie thanked the sergeant for the information he did give her. She also promised him that she would follow-up on his suggestion to visit Police Headquarters and talk with a detective about how investigations were conducted before she wrote the story for her school paper. (*Another reporter's white lie* was again the thought on Angie's mind when she made such a promise.) During her conversation with the police sergeant the items Angie assumed were hard facts she listed in her reporter's note-pad. There were three items she felt were of real significance that she put into her notebook:

1. The police believed the video was a hoax or a joke made by some computer geek.
2. The TV station failed to get the name, address, or telephone number from the person who dropped off the video at the station, and they did not get it when the person later phoned with the additional information.
3. The video clip needed analysis by experts at a laboratory to determine if it was genuine or a computer-made fake, and that had to be done by an out-of-area lab so no results are expected for at least two weeks.

Angie now made some final preparations that were needed to carry out the next steps in her investigation plan. She took her bicycle from the garage and stashed it behind a bush in the backyard where it could not be seen in the dark or from any of the windows in the house. Next, she emptied her backpack of anything in it that would not be absolutely necessary for school the next day. The items she removed were replaced with these: a flashlight; her reporter's notebook; her camera checked to make sure it was loaded with film; her Dad's binoculars which she borrowed from the storage closet where he kept his bird-watching stuff; a piece of fruit and some snack food; a pouch with her fold-up rain cape and hat; and a tightly rolled-up plastic beach mat. Then she laid out the clothes she would need for the morning, and in the pocket of the shirt she was to wear she tucked the miniature tape recorder her Dad gave her after he stopped using it.

When those preparations were finished Angie prepared herself for bed, but before she crawled under the covers there were two final tasks to do. The first was to set her clock radio so it would go on just loud enough to awaken her at 4:30 AM. The second was to write a note that she taped on to the bedroom door of her parents. It said, *Dear Mom and Dad: I forgot to tell you that I needed to get to bed early tonight. Mom, remember I told you that I have a special job to do tomorrow. So don't worry if I'm not here when you wake up in the morning. Don't worry about preparing my bag-lunch. I'll use my allowance money to buy it at the school cafeteria. Good night, I love you, Angie.*

Despite all the excitement and activity of her evening, Angie fell asleep almost as soon as her head hit the pillow. Though her parents and brother arrived home not long after she closed the door to her room and slipped into bed, she was not aware of the jabbering that went on after they all were in the house; nor was she aware that her mother peeked in on her to make sure she was actually there and asleep; neither did she hear the questions Mr. Scrivener kept asking his wife about what his daughter Angie was up to; and, she did not hear anything of the story her mother made up to answer his questions while not giving up the secret she promised Angie she would keep.

CHAPTER 3

▼

FRIDAY BEGINS

Promptly at 4:30 AM the radio switched on, and there were only a few notes of music heard when Angie's hand shot out from the covers to push the off button. It seems that she was fully awake with the first click of the radio switch. She jumped out of bed, threw on her clothes except for shoes which she carried along with her backpack and an outer jacket. She slowly opened her door, tiptoed through the hall and down the stairs to the kitchen. There she carefully opened the back door, put her shoes and the other stuff she was carrying on the stoop. Then she slowly closed the door managing to do it almost with no sound at all.

When she sat down on the top step to put on her shoes she realized that her socks were damp. That was because she forgot that there might be some dampness from the settling of the early morning dew. It was not exactly comfortable, but since there was nothing she could do about it at the moment she got her shoes on over the wet socks. After she donned her jacket and wriggled into her backpack, she retrieved her bike from the bushes where it was stashed and quietly wheeled it through the path in back of their house until she was on the next street.

There she mounted the bike and began to pedal furiously to get away from the neighborhood as soon as possible. She traveled only a few yards when she became aware that there was another matter about which she failed to give proper attention—the seat of her jeans were now wetter than her socks. It had never entered her mind that the bicycle's saddle seat would be soaked from being out in the dampness for so many hours. Wet butt or no wet butt, the icky feeling was ignored for she was determined to keep moving in pursuit of her mission.

As the sky in the east began to turn pink with the rising sun, Angie reached Blossom Avenue. She dismounted from the bike and wheeled it into an alcove next to her favorite ice cream store. At that early hour it was still sheltered from the increasing daylight. Slipping off her backpack, Angie took out the camera and adjusted it so it would be ready to snap a picture of anything coming up or down the street. She crouched in that shadowed niche for almost half an hour, but there was no vehicle of any kind that passed her going in either direction. Indeed, all she saw was a dog sniffing at all the refuse containers it passed hoping to find a tasty morsel.

When she saw a light go on in one of the stores up the street, Angie decided it was time to leave. She was disappointed that the purple mystery automobile, or whatever, did not show up so she could get a photo of it. But she was sure it would never appear when there was activity or other traffic on the street, and that made her certain that it was time to get on with the next phase of her investigation plan. With all her equipment on her back again, she took off on her bike up Blossom Avenue pedaling hard toward the lake.

By the time she reached the entrance to the forest preserve that surrounded the lake her pants and socks were dry, but she was now sweaty from the exertion of a fast two-mile ride. Angie knew when she started out that she would not be able to walk her bike through the heavily wooded area to the spot she intended to set up as her observation post. She did, however, plan in advance for that problem. She remembered many things from when she was in summer day camp with its head-

quarters in the recreation building near the beach. An important recol-
lection for now was the existence of a shallow ravine near the Blossom
Avenue entrance filled with low-growing brush. It was there that she
laid her bike down flat in the brush so it was not visible from the road
or by anyone who might be walking on the forest's foot trails.

Using paths she knew rather than the main entrance road, Angie
now made her way to the line of trees surrounding the edge of the
lake's beach area. She located a spot between two big oak trees whose
trunks were separated by only a foot or so. After laying down her backpack and removing her jacket, she hunted around until she found
enough dead branches to pile up and interweave as a wall between the
two oak trees. It was just tall enough so when she sat or kneeled behind
it her head was below the top. There was enough space between the
branches at her eye level so she could peer out or poke the binoculars
through and get a good view of the whole beach area and a swath of the
lake.

Satisfied that she would not easily be seen behind her makeshift
blind, Angie settled down for what she hoped would be a successful
wait. She emptied her backpack of the special items with which she
stuffed it the night before. With the plastic mat spread out as a ground
cover, she wrapped her jacket around the rain gear pouch and fixed it
so she could sit or kneel on it next to the blind. The binoculars and
camera were placed in easy reach as was her notebook and a pen. With
her preparations completed, Angie sat down on her made-up cushions.
It was then that she was reminded by stomach growls of her missed
breakfast. The growling was a signal that it was time to eat the fruit and
nibble on her snack food.

Her hunger now gone, Angie positioned herself for some concen-
trated watching. She used the binoculars through her peer slot paying
close attention to the line where the sand met the water, and from that
line she would scan a large piece of the lake itself. About thirty minutes
of such careful observation went by, and though Angie alternated

between kneeling and sitting her neck and back muscles were getting tense and beginning to feel sore.

Talking out loud Angie addressed herself, *"Ugh, I must have a little break and take the chance on standing up so I can do some stretching."* She stood erect for a moment or two doing a few stretches and turns. On one of the turns she was looking eastward and noticed that the sun was now above most of the trees in back of her. She was surprised at how rapidly the sun had moved up in the sky, and she quickly dropped to the ground to do some figuring. She looked at her watch and realized that it was almost two hours since she awakened and left her house. After finishing the mental review of her morning's activities and the elapsed time until the present moment, Angie in a raised voice again spoke to herself, *"I can stay today to see if my hunch was a good one only from now until 7:30. I need a good half hour to pack my stuff, get my bike and ride to school. If it doesn't show by then, I'm sure it won't appear when there'll be the possibility of walkers and hikers coming through. Now get back to work, Ms. investigative reporter."*

So Angie settled down at her observation spot again, but this time she kept shifting her position from sitting to kneeling to crouching in order to avoid the strain on her neck and back. Another twenty minutes of her intense watching took place, but now it seemed to Angie as if at least an hour had past.

As the time dragged on, Angie began to have tinges of doubt. Now she was thinking: **Maybe my hunch was all wet, and I'm in the wrong place at the wrong time. Gosh, I'll have a lot of explaining to do at home. Okay, another ten minutes and then I'll quit.**

The time deadline Angie put on herself was getting very close, but then it happened and all her feelings of doubt were immediately gone. About fifty feet out from the water's edge she spotted some ripples on the surface of the water. She dropped the binoculars, grabbed her camera, poked the lens through a separation in the branches and began snapping pictures of the event. The ripples turned into little waves moving toward the shore, and then Angie was sure she saw what appeared to be a glass bubble moving just above the surface of the lake.

As the bubble-like object rose higher above the water, Angie saw that it was larger and rounder than she had expected. It now appeared to her as a dome built into the top of the purple vehicle. Also, as she kept the camera on it taking one picture after another she could see that inside the transparent dome something like a camera with a long telescopic lens was spinning like a top. It fitted the description the caller gave to the TV station before yesterday's evening news telecast. Now Angie could not contain herself. She jumped up to get a better view and to be in a position so that she could more easily swing the camera. That allowed her greater freedom to follow the movement of what she was sure was the purple thing when it emerged from the water and moved onto the beach. She forgot her caution about not being seen or heard, and she practically shouted as she exclaimed, *"Zowie! Wow! It's happening just like I thought it would."*

That outburst was the first giveaway of the fact that she was there and where her observation post was exactly located. The second mistake was something the aspiring reporter never even thought about. By now the sun had risen to a fairly high point in the sky, but all of a sudden it was hidden from view by a passing cloud. It shadowed the spot on which her camera was focused just enough so that the flash went off on one of her snaps. When that happened the bubble-like dome immediately sunk below the surface. There was sort of a little whirlpool, and then the lake was again calm.

Angie was startled by the sudden turn of events, and she reacted by dropping to the ground on her hands and knees. Before she could decide on what she ought to do next, she heard a booming male voice shouting, "The radar eye has pinpointed your location, and I'm coming to get you."

That gave Angie a scare. One thing for certain, she wasn't going to dash for it in an attempt to escape. She took a peek out. Striding on the sand toward her at a very brisk pace was a rather tall man wearing what she thought was a wet suit like underwater divers wore, rubber boots, a helmet of some kind with what looked like a radio antenna attached to it. In his hand he held what appeared to be a computer keyboard. She couldn't tell if he was old or young because his face was covered with one of the wildest, bushiest beards she ever saw. At that instant Angie's desire to be a newspaper reporter overcame her fear. She stood up in full view of the man who was now very close to her. At the same time she shifted her camera into position and took a head-to-toe photo of him.

MR. JACOBSEN DISCOVERS ANGIE'S HIDING PLACE AND BECKONS HER TO COME OUT INTO THE OPEN

In a rather threatening tone of voice, the man spoke to her, "Well now, you are a smart one, and fearless too. Now come out from behind that blind so I can get a good look at you." Angie securely strapped the camera around her neck and under her arm, and she quickly felt her pants pocket to make sure the tape recorder was still there. Then she stepped outside of the blind to face the man whom she knew was the solution to the purple mystery automobile—or whatever it was.

"My name is Angie Inkster Scrivener. I live in Plainview, and I am a fifth grader in our elementary school. This morning I came here because I'm working on a news story so I can become the community Junior Reporter for the MORNING HERALD. I hope you will help me. Will you, please?" Angie blurted this out very loudly and clearly as if she were making a speech of some sort in front of an audience rather than just to a person standing right in front of her.

"That's a very eloquent speech," the man said to her, "but there is no need to shout. I definitely do not have a hearing problem."

"Please excuse me, Mister, I didn't mean to shout. I guess my excitement got the best of me."

"It's Mister Jacobsen, that's with an e before the n. I may look a little wild and crazy, but I'm not going to bite you," he told Angie. "I must tell you, Miss Scrivener, I was expecting someone to find out about me and my invention. In fact, I was rather hoping it would happen soon, but I didn't think it would be this soon. And I certainly never thought it would be a brash, little school girl who must be very clever."

"Thank you, Mr. Jacobsen with an e, but you didn't answer my question."

"I didn't forget, I was thinking it over," Mr. Jacobsen responded, "Listen, young lady, I'll make you a trade. I'll tell you what you want to know, if you'll answer some questions for me."

"Yes sir, that's a deal. Just let me put my stuff together, and we'll go over and sit on the sand in the sun where we can do our interviews."

"My goodness you surely do talk like a reporter already, but there's a better place for us than the beach. Gather your things up, and we shall converse in the comfort of Jacob Jacobsen's multipurpose vehicle. No one will see us while we're in the deep."

"Golleee, Mr. Jacobsen, sir, thanks a lot. What a scoop for my first published newspaper article."

For an instant all the rules she was taught at home and in school about accepting offers of rides or gifts from strangers flitted through Angie's mind. At this moment, though, she was certain that it was important to see the inside of the purple vehicle if she were going to get all the facts she needed to write her winning news story. She was completely confident that there would be no danger in going off with this strange-looking man in his very peculiar contraption.

ANGIE AS SHE COMES OUT FROM HER HIDING PLACE
MAKING SURE SHE HAS HER CAMERA,
TAPE RECORDER AND NOTE PAD

CHAPTER 4

▼

FRIDAY MORNING ON
THE JACOBSEN

Mr. Jacobsen waited until Angie put everything in her backpack except her camera, notepad and pen. Then they walked together toward the water's edge. As they proceeded Angie noticed that Mr. Jacobsen bent his head toward the lake and punched in some signals on the keyboard-like thing he held in one hand while he worked the keys with the other. Seconds after he touched his fingers to the keys, the transparent dome poked through the water and began moving to the shoreline. Angie asked if it was made of glass.

"Oh my, no ma'am," Mr. Jacobsen answered, "I couldn't possibly shape glass like that by myself. It's Plexiglas, a plastic you can mold with heat."

Angie managed to jot down "dome, Plexiglas, mold" on her pad even as she kept her eyes glued on the movement of what she now knew was correctly called a multipurpose vehicle. "And what's the thing going round and round in the Plexiglas dome?" she asked.

"Why it's just a simple device I invented to give the vehicle eyes and ears. It's a combination of a radio receiver, a radar device, a camera and a computer. But I'll explain all the electronics and the machinery when we're inside THE JACOBSEN."

There was no chance for Angie to make a note of what was just explained to her because at that moment THE JACOBSEN, as Mr. Jacobsen just referred to it, reached shallow water and its sleek, purple body became visible. Angie Inkster's eyes opened wide and her jaw dropped as the vehicle approached the shoreline.

Mr. Jacobsen must have tapped some keys on his keyboard while she wasn't looking. Apparently that sent out another signal from his helmet antenna because a small door opened on the front of the vehicle and a metal arm shot out from the opening. It extended itself like a telescope when its several sections are pulled out to make it longer. Attached to the end of the arm was a mechanical claw. Its metal fingers opened up and dug into the sand until they were as far as they could go, and then as the steel arm became shorter THE JACOBSEN was pulled up onto the beach.

It took a second for Angie to get over her surprise, then she whipped out her camera; however, before she pressed the shutter button she turned to Mr. Jacobsen and asked, "May I take a picture, sir?"

"Yes, yes, but hurry, we must get in and under the water before someone else spots us."

Completely on dry land now the very purple multipurpose vehicle named THE JACOBSEN moved on its ordinary looking automobile wheels to where they were standing. On the side facing them a door hinged at its top opened and a set of stairs as on a commuter airplane dropped down to the ground. Mr. Jacobsen snatched up the backpack when it slipped from Angie's shoulder as she took the picture of the vehicle climbing on to the shore. He then herded her up the stairs into THE JACOBSEN climbing in right behind her. The door folded shut, and immediately the vehicle was again in motion.

Once inside Angie took a quick look around. There was no outside light coming in because, as she expected would be the case, there were no windows of any kind. The room was bathed in a soft glow of dim light from a panel on the ceiling. In addition there was reflected light from a big television screen that took up a whole wall on what Angie assumed was the front of the vehicle. On the screen the whole beach-front with the forest in the background was visible, and she could see the arm and its claw now pushing the Jacobsen multipurpose vehicle into the water.

Mr. Jacobsen was now seated at a small desk in the middle of the room that Angie could see was furnished like the salon or cabin of a big pleasure boat. There were many plush, comfortable chairs placed around several small round tables all with a series of colored buttons inserted in the center of their tops. Angie went behind Mr. Jacobsen to look at what was on the desk on which his eyes seemed to be riveted. She realized that he was looking at a computer monitor built into a well of the desk, and to the right of it was also a big keyboard. There were numerous symbols flashing across the screen and what looked to her like geography maps.

Sensing that Angie was about to ask a question, Mr. Jacobsen spoke first: "I'll be with you in a few minutes, Miss Scrivener. Keep yourself occupied here in the management station module while I program the vehicle for our underwater stay. Incidentally, do you have any other appointments this morning?"

Angie by this time was so absorbed in what was now a great adven-ture that her deadline for starting back to school was completely for-gotten. She glanced at her watch and then said to Mr. Jacobsen, "I was hoping to get to school by 8:00 AM, but I guess I'll never make it now. It's okay, I'll just have to be late, this is worth it, but if you could get me back to the beach in not much more than an hour I would appreci-ate it. And please, sir, call me Angie, not Ms. Scrivener."

"No problem, Angie. And you can call me by my first name. It's Jacob, and it's with an o before the b. Now don't giggle, Jacob Jacob-sen is not any stranger than Angie Inkster Scrivener."

Angie found a chair near one of the little tables, placed her reporter's notepad on the table and began making a diagram of what she now knew was the management station module. She cast her eyes about the room to see the layout and where the various pieces of furniture and other objects were placed, and then she sketched them in on her diagram. The giant TV had grown dark as THE JACOBSEN moved away from the shore, but as her glance came to that wall she noticed that there was a picture being displayed again. A very strong light was beaming out from the vehicle, and a big underwater section of the lake appeared to be bathed in bright sunlight. There were fish swimming around, a lot of different colored plants that Angie never knew grew in the lake, and all sorts of water life that were crawling around in the mud or resting on crags of rocks that stuck up from the lake bottom. Angie just stared in wonderment forgetting even to write in her notepad what she was seeing.

At the control module Mr. Jacobsen finished his tasks, he stood up and walked over to the back of the chair on which Angie was seated. He quietly watched what she was doing. He didn't speak until he noticed her reaction at what she saw on the television wall. Angie was startled when he said to her, "It is beautiful, this is one of my favorite underwater viewing spots. This is the lake's deepest water, and it is a place where I can park THE JACOBSEN and not worry about it being discovered."

Angie's mind was practically bursting with questions, and she started with a big one first, "Mr. Jacobsen, why…."

She never had the chance to finish the asking of her question because Mr. Jacobsen interrupted her, "No more questions from you at this time, young lady. Remember our deal. I interview you first, and then you can shower me with questions if I'm convinced you will be giving me honest answers." With that he drew up a chair and sat facing Angie on the other side of the little table.

"I'm ready," Angie told him, "fire away Mr. Jacobsen with an e between the s and the n."

"I like that, young'un, you have a nice sense of humor and a good memory. Now, first question: Who else knows you were staking me out?"

"No one, Mr. Jacobsen, I snuck out of my house at 4:30 this morning. My mother knows that there was some investigation I intended in order to discover a story for my HERALD Junior Reporter competition entry. But I'm sure she has no idea of where I am or what sort of a story I was after."

"Second question: Are you fronting for someone—that is, did some adult person ask you to do this for pay or something?"

Angie was annoyed that Mr. Jacobsen thought she might be lying to him, and she showed it when she said, "Listen here Jacob Jacobsen, I've told some reporter's white lies to get some information I needed to develop my hunch. But I made a deal with you when we were on the beach, and deals mean promises that you can't take back."

"That's a very sharp response Angie Inkster Scrivener, but you are quite right about a deal being like a contract. I believe you, but I did need to know that you are on your own. There are a few people who know about my invention, and I think there is a plot to steal it from me before it has patent protection. I expect to hear from Washington about the approval of my application within the next day or two."

"Wow, this story has a lot more to it than I ever expected," Angie exclaimed. "Is it my turn to ask the questions now?"

"Almost," answered THE Jacobsen's inventor, "but I'm curious about how you came to your hunch to look for me out here. I suppose it started with your seeing the video of the vehicle on the TV news, but others saw it too and I'm sure there was a police report. You seemed to figure out what kind of a vehicle it was and where to locate it almost immediately."

"Well, not exactly in a flash," Angie told him, "but it didn't take very long. Two thoughts hit me when I first saw what the newsperson said was a purple automobile flash across the screen. First, it occurred to me that it might be a boat of some sort, because there was a vision in my mind of seeing a sleek-shaped purplish kind of boat on the lake during one summer. Second, the thought came to me that it couldn't be just a boat. That happened when I heard that the call-in person said he saw no windows."

"So far I would say that your thinking was in the right channel," commented Mr. Jacobsen. "But tell me, what made you think it might be a machine that could go underwater?"

To answer his question Angie told him, "That was easy. When I saw it on the TV news report last evening, it reminded me of a submarine. It had no windows or portholes, its shape was similar to submarine pictures I've seen, and I thought the thing in the dome on top was like a periscope. Besides, there had to be some reason it was traveling on Blossom Avenue in the direction of the lake."

Now it was Mr. Jacobsen's turn for an exclamation: "By *gad, dagummit* for a fifth grader you are some whippersnapper! You are going to make some hotshot reporter. Is there more to this detective work of yours?"

Angie then told him about her calls to the police and to the TV station, and why from the information she got she was sure about several matters that strengthened her hunch. "I came to the conclusion," she explained, "that the vehicle was being operated remotely, that the video was not a fake or computer generated by some whiz kid. I also figured that whoever was sending the signals to the speeding purple thing was the one who made the video, brought it to the station and phoned in the additional information."

"You were absolutely on track, and I couldn't believe that in both instances the receptionist never asked me to identify myself. Of course, if I were asked, I would not have given a true answer. Okay, Angie, it's your interview now."

Angie was more than ready with her questions, but there was a request to make first: "May I use my little recorder to get the questions and answers on tape? It will make writing story easier, and it will be more accurate than just using my handwritten notes.

Mr. Jacobsen did not object to the use of the tape recorder, so Angie removed it from her pocket, switched it to record and placed it on the table between them. "I'm ready to begin," she said, "and here's my first question: What is your age and how long have you been a resident of this area?"

Mr. Jacobsen answered that question and a bunch of others giving Angie all the information she needed for her story. Everything she asked and all of the answers given to her questions were recorded on the tape. She now knew a lot of personal things about Jacob Jacobsen: that he was old enough to be her grandfather; that he was a widower with no children; that he was born on a farm right here at the edge of the forest preserve; and, that he came back to live in the old farmhouse only a year ago when he retired from his job as a mechanical equipment design engineer for a firm in California.

One of the important questions Angie posed to Mr. Jacobsen was: "What made you decide to build a machine like this, and where did you get all the parts?"

The response the inventor with the big, bushy beard gave to that inquiry struck Angie as amazing and funny at the same time. He told her that after his parents died he inherited the farm, but since he was working so far away he asked his uncle to live there and keep an eye on the place. By that time it was no longer a working farm because much of the land was sold to people for building lots. The uncle took care of all the subdividing and selling until he died, and that is when Mr. Jacobsen retired and came back to the home where he lived until as a young man he went off to his job in the west. He found the house in good repair, and he discovered that his uncle had kept up the old barn with his old workshop things, his sleek purple racing boat and even his first automobile that he believed his father sent to the junkyard ages ago.

Mr. Jacobsen's exact words as captured on the tape were:

"And that's how I got started to invent and build **THE JACOB-SEN.** When I saw all that stuff in our old barn, I knew immediately what my retirement project was going to be. You see, the idea for a multipurpose vehicle like this was in my head for a long time, but whenever I proposed it to the directors of my company they didn't think it could be made cheap enough to be sold at a profit. That old boat and car are actually parts of this vehicle in one form or another, other parts I made myself or picked up in junkyards or in computer stores."

Among her many other interview questions, Angie wanted to know why he said when he first found her at her hiding place that he expected to be found, but not so soon. To that query he explained that when he was sure his patent was approved, he needed to find some bank or a group of investors who would finance the manufacture of multipurpose vehicles based on THE JACOBSEN model. He explained to Angie that there were many commercial uses for such a vehicle, and he believed he knew how to produce them at reasonable cost.

Angie's last question for Mr. Jacobsen was: "Why did you go to all that trouble of making the video and taking the chance of speeding **THE JACOBSEN** up Blossom Avenue that way, especially since you were worried about the people who wanted to steal it?"

"Oh, I can answer that, and first you should know that what I did was no mistake. Yep, there was a good reason for my risky actions, and I'll tell you about that reason," said the inventor as he shook the fingers of his free hand in Angie's face. "It was the first step in my plan for stirring up a mystery. I hoped the mystery would make for a lot of news either when my project was discovered or when I went public with it. I figured it would help a lot in getting the attention of the investors I needed."

At this point Angie felt that she was now in possession of all the information she needed to write the news story for submission to the HERALD. She clicked off the tape recorder and said, "It was cool, sir, my first interview as a reporter. I thank you very much Jacob Jacobsen, the inventor of this terrific purple multipurpose vehicle appropriately named, THE JACOBSEN."

There was a booming laugh from Mr. Jacobsen. Then he responded to Angie by saying, "Well, you're a cool kid, Angie Inkster, so it was a cool interview. And I would like from this day on to be your cool friend too, so from now on I'm just Jacob to you. Now, are you sure there are no more questions before I take you down below to show you all the machinery that makes it possible for us to stay underwater and still have plenty of good breathing air?"

"No, not exactly," Angie answered, "but there is another deal I'd like to make with you."

"I'm listening, young'un. What's your proposal?" Angie then explained to him that the HERALD would not publish the name of the Junior Reporter selected by the judges and print that person's winning news story until thirteen more days had passed. Speaking with great confidence she said, "Now there is no question about the fact that I will be selected for that job, and I'm sure that when my story is printed it will create a lot of excitement and a bunch of publicity for you. Please, sir, I mean Jacob with an o, could you lay low and keep THE JACOBSEN hidden somehow until after the HERALD announces the winner of the competition?"

"It's a done deal, Angie. It might be difficult, but I'll do it. By then the publicity will be good, and I'll be able to announce that THE JACOBSEN has patent protection. C'mon, we just have time for a quick tour of the machinery module below."

Angie noticed that right before Mr. Jacobsen left the table where they both were sitting during the interviewing, he quickly punched some of the table's colored buttons. She saw, too, that as they passed the control desk he stopped to look at the computer monitor for a moment. Anxious to see the rest of THE JACOBSEN and with ideas going through her mind about how she would write her story, Angie didn't give a thought to what Mr. Jacobsen was doing. When they were down in the machinery module, though, she began to feel as if her new friend Jacob was in a big hurry with his descriptions of the stuff in the machinery module. She also realized that he was doing something she hadn't seen him do before—he was constantly stroking his beard.

"Jacob," she said, "I know it's more than an hour since we got here. Remember, I did tell you that it was okay for me to get to school late today. I'll probably have some detention, but believe me everything will be okay. So don't worry about it"

"Angie, I'm sorry to say you have it wrong this time. I'm not concerned about your being late getting back to school, I'm worried about your getting there at all."

That was something Angie never even thought about as a possibility, and her voice was more than a little tense when she spoke, "What? What do you mean, why not? What if my parents discover that I did not attend school today?"

"Don't fret about that because we are equipped for both telephone and radio communication. If it becomes necessary we will use it, and I assure you that storm, or no storm, we will be quite safe and snug here. There will also be plenty to eat if required."

The news about being able to call home or radio for help if it were required calmed Angie down some, and the edge on her voice was gone when she next spoke. "What storm? And if there is going to be one how do you know about it? And if you did know, why didn't you tell me about it before now?"

"Whoa there, friend, stop spitting out one question after another so I'll have a chance to give some answers. Apparently you haven't been aware that THE JACOBSEN has been shifting around some. A strong wind started blowing just when you were offering me that last deal. I don't know if it's just temporary, or if it means a big storm is on its way. Let's get up to the management station module, and we'll check things out."

The first thing Angie noticed when they mounted the gangway and stepped into the upper deck module, was the view on the big wall screen. It was clear that they were not in the same position as before, and she could see that there seemed to be a strong current in the water.

Mr. Jacobsen went right over to the computer console, and after some fast use of the keyboard he peered at the monitor very intently. "Look here," he said to Angie, "I've patched in to the weather service's satellite pictures. We're in luck because the wind is down. The radar images do show storm clouds moving in, but it will be at least an hour before they reach this vicinity."

Angie was then told to get all her things together and to get everything stuffed into her backpack except her jacket, which she should start wearing immediately. She did, and as she packed all her other belongings she saw that Mr. Jacobsen was putting on his funny helmet and strapping on the portable keyboard he was using when he first moved THE JACOBSEN to the beach area. He then came over to her to make sure her backpack would not slip from her shoulders.

"Okay, everything is programmed so we're leaving our submerged position, and rising to the surface. Once on top the air pumps will stop and you will hear the woosh of a jet stream in the water, and then we'll be moving in boat mode toward the shore. Ill explain the rest when we get below."

Back down in the machinery module, Mr. Jacobsen guided Angie to where the telescopic arm with its claws on one end was resting on a track built into the floor. Mr. Jacobsen pressed a button or flipped a switch nearby and the claw turned so that its fingers reached upward and was shaped into the form of a basket. Angie sort of knew what was going to happen. She soon discovered how right she was as soon as Mr. Jacobsen started speaking to her.

"Angie, my friend, listen to these instructions carefully. I'm going to pick you up and place you in the center of the upturned claw. Sit or crouch down as low as you can. In about thirty seconds we will be as close to the shore as the shallow water will allow. The two small doors in front of you will swing open and the arm will begin to extend until the claw is over a dry part of the beach. Then I'll give the signal for it to be lowered, and I'll swivel it so that you will slide out and be deposited on the sand. Then get up and run off the beach as fast as you can. Don't be scared everything will go smoothly. I designed THE JACOB-SEN so it could be used for rescue missions like this."

Angie told him that she was not scared, but that she was worried about his safety and their not being spotted with the vehicle on top of the water. He explained that he would back up and submerge very rapidly and maneuver the vehicle back to its underwater berth. "Then I'll wait out the storm, and after dark I'll put on my diving gear and swim underwater to the far cove, and from there it's only a short walk to the house. Here you go."

Before she could say anything, Angie was swept up in Jacob Jacobsen's arms and set down inside the claw. The doors opened, the metal arm slid forward on its track until she and the claw were outside and in the daylight. Gently but very quickly the arm was extended until the claw was over the beach. Just before she was dumped to the ground, Mr. Jacobsen shouted one last instruction. It was that when she was safely off the beach she should look for something in her jacket pocket.

Angie never even felt the swiveling motion of the claw before it opened and allowed her to gently slide onto the ground. Then the fingers of the claws quickly closed up, and the arm to which it was attached became shorter and shorter as the back end of it moved through the open clam doors into the vehicle's machinery module. Angie raced toward what earlier was her observation post. The blind she constructed from the branches was still intact.

She ducked behind it and sat down for a moment to catch her breath, and she fished in her jacket pockets to find whatever was supposed to be there. What she found was a piece of paper with some numbers on the top and a few words scrawled beneath them. This is what Angie read: *Here's a phone number where I can be reached wherever I am. Try* to *let me know that you reached school safely. You can call me any time you think it is important. Please don't give anybody the number or tell anyone where I am until after your story is in the HERALD. Your new friend, Jacob*

Angie shoved the note into her pocket and scurried off to find her bike.

CHAPTER 5

▼

STILL FRIDAY: ANGIE MAKES IT TO SCHOOL

Angie did not have any difficulty finding the brush-filled ravine where her bike was hidden. She could tell from the bike's condition that there were strong winds blowing during the last part of her stay on THE JACOBSEN. A lot of sand and stuff was blown around during the high winds. Some of the windblown sand and damp leaves covered the bike seat and parts of the handlebars. Angie picked it up, shook off some of the messy stuff and walked it over to the road. Once on the road's hard surface she hopped on, rode out to Blossom Avenue in a standing position so she could get extra power when she pushed on the pedals.

In record time she came to the main part of town. It was quite different than when she left there early that morning. Now the streets and sidewalks were not empty. There was plenty of traffic, and there were throngs of people moving about still getting to work or out for early shopping. *"Oh, oh,"* Angie said to herself, *"I can't ride through on the street with that* traffic, *and I'll be too obvious if I wheel the bike along on the sidewalk."* Then a really dark thought crossed her mind: *Dang,*

dang, darn! This is the day I heard Dad say the students in one of his classes would be downtown doing a traffic study as a special project. What if he's out with them and he sees me. That I can't risk because he'd never believe why I was getting to school so late.

Even though it would take several minutes longer for her to get to school, Angie decided a detour was in order. She made a U turn and retraced her route for several blocks. After a couple of wrong turns, she found a street that allowed her to make a big loop around the Plainview business district. When she finally reached the part of the schoolyard where the bike rack was located, she parked her bike and began racing across the yard to the closest entrance.

At the doorway she stopped before opening the doors to look at her watch. Again she talked out loud to herself: *"Holy Cow, it's almost ten o'clock, I might as well go right to the office. I'm sure my teacher will not let me just march into class at this hour. But what kind of excuse am I going to use for being so late. Well, it might as well be a big lie, because it will only be a temporary one until everybody learns the truth."*

Apparently the needed excuse popped right into her mind because she pulled open the door and walked swiftly to the main office. Once inside she finally unhitched her backpack. Stuffed as it was, Angie now realized how heavy it felt. Not only that, Mr. Jacobsen had bound it on so securely that some of the straps were painfully digging into her. When the burden of the backpack was shed, she approached the counter where the school secretary, Mrs. Penner, was already giving her stern looks.

"My goodness, Ms. Scrivener," she said in a very formal way, "you're rather disheveled and certainly a little grimy. I suppose your excuse for being so late is that you encountered some gang on the way to school, were beaten up and needed to stop for emergency medical treatment. Is that it?"

"No ma'am, not exactly," Angie answered.

"And what is exactly, young lady?"

"I did have an accident. You see, I rode my bike today so I could do an errand on the way here. All of a sudden a squirrel ran right in front of me and I swerved to avoid it. I guess I swerved too hard because my bike jumped the curb crossed over the sidewalk and crashed into a big row of bushes. I landed in the bushes with the bike on top of me."

All those words flowed from Angie's tongue like a swift current. Then she paused for a second to think of what she was supposed to say next. Mrs.Penner took advantage of the momentary silence saying, "Oh, that's when you were injured and required an ambulance." Clearly, she was not yet convinced Angie was giving her a true story.

Ignoring Mrs. Penner's skeptical remark, Annie continued with her version of what happened, "I didn't think I was hurt, but the problem was I couldn't get up. The bicycle was tangled in the bushes and my backpack straps were snarled on some part of the bike. I just couldn't free myself. So I started calling for help. Nobody came, and I guess I was hidden from the view of the few cars that came up the street."

This time she kept talking as fast as she could so that Mrs. Penner would not interrupt until finished. "I lay sprawled there on my back for some time. Finally, a very old lady came by from a nearby house and untangled me. She was a little deaf so she never heard my cries for help. I tried to thank her and leave, but she insisted I come into her house so I could wash my face and hands. Then she insisted I have a cup of tea. I told her several times I was in a hurry to get to school, but I don't think she heard anything right except my name. That bothers me because I'm afraid she might look up our number, call my Mom and tell her that her daughter was in an accident. May I please use the phone to call home, because if the nice old lady did call then my mother will be worried?"

When Mrs. Penner heard that Angie wanted to call home, she thought that perhaps Angie was telling a true story. So she gave permission for Angie to use the office phone. Angie quickly punched in a number, but it wasn't the Scrivener's phone number. It was the number Mr. Jacobsen wrote at the top of his note, which was already fixed in Angie's memory. When the call she placed was answered, what Mrs. Penner heard Angie say was: "Mom, it's Angie, I'm at school No, I'm not sick, everything is okay, but in case you received a call that I was in an accident on the way to school I just wanted you to know it was just a tumble. I was very late in getting here so I'll need a note from you tomorrow Yes, I'll be home on time.... Don't worry, I'll be very careful."

Angie knew that Mr. Jacobsen would understand the message, and Mrs. Penner was now convinced that Angie's unusual excuse was probably true. She did not say anything about seeing the principal and a lateness detention. After a class admittance pass was completed, the only thing Mrs. Penner said to Angie was, "I advise you to get your clothes brushed off some and your hair combed before your teacher and your classmates see you."

That advice Angie did heed. After a last glance in the bathroom mirror showed that her appearance was somewhat improved, she proceeded to her classroom. Her entrance to the room happened to be a very dramatic one, because at that moment Jacob Jacobsen's predicted storm swept into Plainview. There was crash of thunder and flashes of lightning that brightened the now darkened room as she walked to the teacher's desk and placed Mrs. Penner's pass on it.

Naturally there was a lot of buzzing and whispering as Angie reached her row and settled down at her own desk. The teacher wrapped on the chalkboard with her pointer for quiet, and went right on with her lesson about geography and the settlement of the West. She completely ignored Angie's tardy arrival and the raging storm.

Angie tried to listen carefully to what Ms. Rivers was explaining, but her usual attention was lagging. She was having visions of the almost unimaginable events of the morning. Also on her mind was how she was going to handle lunchtime. She knew that once she was sitting with her usual tablemates there would be a deluge of questions about her appearance and late arrival. And that is exactly what happened, with her friend Nancy giving her the worst grilling. Angie repeated the excuse she told Mrs. Penner as the reason for her tardiness, but Nancy had more doubts about it than anybody.

She realized that in some way she must get Nancy to stop pressuring her, Angie decided to take the chance that their long friendship would payoff. She put her mouth to Nancy's ear and whispered, "Quit being so dorky. If you're my friend, stop encouraging everyone into believing I'm lying. Keep your mouth closed for a few days, then I'll share something with you that will be the best school newspaper story lead you'll ever have."

That did the trick. Nancy made a motion like she was turning the key on her mouth to lock it. Then she shuffled her lunch leavings and garbage onto her tray and marched off to dispose of it saying, "We have a math quiz this afternoon, and I can use a little study time." Everyone at the table followed her in short order.

Angie made it through the afternoon without suffering further bugging since the various class assignments kept everyone busy. When the last bell sounded, she managed to reach her locker very fast. She grabbed her jacket and backpack, slammed the locker door shut, snapped the lock and dashed off to the bike rack. Fortunately, their math teacher for some reason detained Nancy, so she wasn't around to pounce on her again.

By dismissal time the storm was over and it was again clear and sunny. Among the other things on Angie's mind was the unhappy prospect of either waiting out the storm or riding home in a thunderstorm. Since the storm did subside, she was able to make one quick stop on the way home. That was to pull her camera from the backpack, unload the exposed roll of film and drop it off for developing and printing.

Once in the garage to put her bike in its ordinary parking place she breathed a sigh of relief and enjoyed some comfortable thoughts: *Thank goodness it's Friday. I'll be able to spend most of the weekend work-*

ing on the news story. And I don't see Mom or Dad's car or Benjee's bike.
Good, I'll have the house to myself long enough to put back Dad's binocu-
lars, take a shower and put on some presentable clothes for our Sabbath eve
family dinner.

Mrs. Scrivener worked part time as a social worker at the local hospital, usually on Friday afternoons she was home long before Angie
would get there. Today there was a delay because of a problem with a
patient. As a result when she did get home she found that Angie was
already setting the table for their Sabbath dinner. All day she was anxious about what her daughter was up to that required such an early
morning departure without breakfast and leaving behind an unmade
bed. Now she was going to have her chance to ask some questions
while the two of them were alone.

"Thank you, Angie dear, for getting started on things for dinner. I
hope that isn't a payback for what you did not do this morning."

"Mom, I know I have a lot of explaining to do, and I do thank you
for giving me cover from Dad last night."

"Your welcome, Angie, but if there's a lot of explaining to do, I'm
listening."

Angie didn't tell her mother everything about her long and eventful
day. She asked her Mom to understand that she would still have to
keep a part of her day secret until her HERALD competition story
entry was published. That she spent most of the morning out at the
lake, she did tell. There was also an explanation about her lateness in
getting to school, and the awful story she made up about the reasons
for her tardiness. She realized that Benjee might have learned about
that episode from one of her classmates. If so, she thought her mother
should hear her version in advance.

Mrs. Scrivener was not particularly thrilled with the sparse details
Angie offered about her day's activities. She did promise that she
would be patient until she heard the whole story, and that she would
keep the secret about Angie's Junior Reporter aspirations. Her last

comment before Mr. Scrivener and Benjee arrived was, "I'll deal with your father, but you are on your own with your brother."

After the blessings over the wine and the special Sabbath braided bread, there were no unexpected happenings during dinner. Fatigue, though, was catching up with Angie, and every so often she seemed to nod off. Benjee noticed that and he right away called it to his mother's attention, "Ma, look at the brat, she is actually sleeping through Sabbath dinner."

Mrs. Scrivener didn't respond, but Mr. Scrivener said to Benjee, "And you, young man, are violating the Sabbath referring to your sister in that way." Then he turned to Angie and asked, "You're not coming down with something, are you?"

Ignoring his father's reprimand, Benjee interrupted before Angie could answer her father's question, "Of course she's sick, Dad. Haven't you noticed how quiet it has been all evening? We didn't have any of her usual non-stop talkie-talk-talk all evening."

Benjee knew it was time to shut up by the glare he got from his Dad. Angie was about to deliver a nasty remark to her brother, but at the moment her mother interrupted. "Angie Inkster," she said, "It has been a very long day for you because of that early errand you did for me. I think you're sleepy, so I am excusing you to go up to your room and rest. Benjee will do the cleanup chores tonight."

Benjee started to open his mouth in protest. Again, a stern glare from his Dad convinced him not to say the words.

Angie put her napkin on the table and slunk out of the room. As she began her climb up the stairs to her room, she turned toward the dining room and blew a silent kiss in her Mom's direction.

CHAPTER 6

▼

AT THE SCRIVENER'S HOUSE: THE SABBATH AND SUNDAY

The following morning the sun beaming down on her face awakened Angie. When her eyes opened she knew it must be very late because it was rare that the sun shone through her windows during the morning hours. She looked at her clock radio, and was shocked by the time it showed—it was almost noon. She threw off the covers and jumped out of bed. In a matter of minutes she was dressed, carefully made her bed and did a fast pickup of items strewn about so the room was made to look reasonably neat.

Two important matters she did attend to before she left her room. The first was to check out her backpack to make sure her brother did not do any snooping during her sound morning sleep. She was satisfied that was not the case, but as a precaution she removed the tape recorder and her notepad. There was one desk drawer that could be locked with a key. That is where she put those two items, and when the drawer was locked she hung the key around her neck with it hidden under her blouse.

The second matter was to retrieve Mr. Jacobsen's note that was still crumpled up in the pocket of her jacket from yesterday. Positive that she would not forget the phone number, she tore the paper into tiny bits and discarded them in the wastebasket. Now she was ready to eat and discover what was going on in the house.

When she came to the bottom of the stairs, Angie noticed that the place was very quiet. A quick look around convinced her that at the moment she was the only occupant. In the kitchen she found a note from her mother.

It said: *Angie, your father and Benjee went to Synagogue. Benjee will go right to a friend's house after services and will be sleeping over. Dad is going to visit grandma at the nursing home, and won't be home until late this afternoon. I was needed at the hospital to help with the family of a man waiting for a heart transplant. There's plenty of food, but do not, I repeat, do not leave the house until I return.*
Love,
Mom.

The good news in the message was that Benjee would not be home most of the weekend to annoy her or to destroy her concentration with his constant bouncing of the basketball under her window. The bad news was about the man waiting for a transplant. She was sorry for the family, but she was aware that those cases upset her Mom and often kept her away for many hours.

It was now twelve thirty and Angie was starving. She decided to make herself a brunch—to her that meant eating lunch and breakfast at the same time. She made a terrific spread for herself. She ate leisurely while she turned the pages of the morning paper making sure there were no stories about any one who might have seen the mystery vehicle. There were none, she was still in luck. When Angie finished her brunch meal, she quickly put the kitchen back in order. The table was cleared, the dirty dishes and utensils rinsed and loaded in the dishwasher. It was now 1:30, and satisfied that she was leaving the kitchen at least as neat as she found it, Angie marched up to her room ready to start work on THE JACOBSEN story.

Once in her room Angie removed the tape recorder from the locked desk drawer. She knew it had an earphone jack and she rummaged through her closet until she found a set of earphones. Once everything was set up with earphones plugged in and the tape rewound, she found a comfortable position on her bed and listened to a run through of the interview. She listened to it over and over again until she was sure that all the facts she could use were totally in her head. Then she took her notepad from the drawer, and this time sitting on the floor she read and reread her notes that helped to fix in her mind all the details of her investigation. A complete outline of the story was now in her head, and there was only one task remaining before her actual writing could begin. That was a review of all the photos to decide how she would refer to them in her story.

Her clock radio now showed that it was near four o'clock. Just as she was wondering how she would be able to get to the photo store to pick up her films she heard the garage door open. Sure that it was her Mom, she first scooped up the remainder of her last week's allowance from her nightstand, and then she hurried down the stairs. She reached the front door just as Mrs. Scrivener opened it.

"Hi, Mom, how did it go?" As she asked the question Angie could see that her mother was weary, because she didn't respond. What she did do was drop her portfolio on the entrance hall table, and immediately get to the nearest soft chair where she flopped down. Then she looked at her daughter and said, "I think I'm as tired as you looked last night. Did you get some rest?"

"Mom, I rested alright. I didn't get up until almost noon, and then I made myself a great brunch. I'm fine."

"I'm glad," was her mother's brief comment. Then she asked, "Angie dear, do you think you could rustle me up a cup of tea and an apple? I'll have that and then go up and lie down for a bit."

Angie hurried into the kitchen to prepare what her mother requested. In a few minutes she was back with the tea and fixings along with the apple on a small plate, the needed utensils along with pretty napkin all nicely arranged on a tray. She received a nice compliment from her mother.

While her Mom was drinking her tea, Angie told her how she spent the afternoon getting ready to start the writing of her story. Then she asked, "Would it be okay if I took a bike ride just in the neighborhood? I've been in all day, and I could use some fresh air. I'll be back long before its dark, could I Mom, please?" Mrs. Scrivener just nodded indicating that permission was granted. Angie rushed to the garage, hopped on her bike and was off to the photo store.

Anxious as she was to see the prints of yesterday's picture taking, Angie was careful not to open the film package in the store to take a quick look. That was her usual procedure whenever she would pick up any developed film. Her caution this time was dictated by her fear that the store clerk or another customer looking over her shoulder might get a glimpse of her shot of THE JACOBSEN emerging from the lake onto the shore. At that moment it dawned on her that she neglected to think of the chance she took of blowing the news about her discovery before her story was even written. The risk she forgot to take into account was that the photo store technician who operated the developing and printing equipment might have selected one of her key photos to examine. But apparently that did not happen, and as Angie hastily left the store she breathed a sigh of relief for that lucky break.

She was lucky again when she got back home. There was no explaining to do about why one of her jean pockets showed such a big bulge. Once inside, the quiet told her that her Mom was probably asleep, and she knew her Dad was not yet home because his car was not in the driveway or in the garage. Not wishing to awaken her Mom and be subject to any questions, she tiptoed up the stairs to her room.

With the door closed she flopped down on the floor, tore open the film package and spread the prints out to see how many were usable. Although some of the shots did not print at all, Angie was pleased at how many were excellent shots. After she carefully inspected them several times, she sorted them into two piles. One of the piles contained only a half dozen pictures. These were the ones she decided could best be used in connection with her story. Those she tucked in to the middle of her notepad, and the others along with all the negatives went into the locked desk drawer.

Angie did a little soft shoe dance, pounded the fist of one hand into the palm of the other several times and made another one of her speeches to herself, "Yes, yes, I'm ready, very ready. Watch out computer, here I come!"

The rest of the weekend was all work for Angie. Her Dad came home about sunset time, and she hardly inquired about her grandmother before she was begging him to have unrestricted use of the computer in his study until Sunday afternoon. She warded off his questions about what the big need was by telling him it was an important school project with a Monday morning deadline. Once in her Dad's study with all her support items, Angie sat down at the computer keyboard and typed in the headline to go with her story: **BLOSSOM AVENUE PURPLE AUTOMOBILE MYSTERY IS SOLVED** For a few seconds Angie intently stared at the screen, and the thought that ran through her head was: *I bet that headline will grab the readers' attention.*

Angie allowed herself only brief moment for self-congratulations, and then she started banging away at the keyboard in earnest. Though she was not yet a typing expert, the words seemed to flow from her head to her fingers as if they were directed to the right keys by some sort of magical force. Every page or so she clicked the "save" button to make sure the work would not get lost or accidentally erased. She would frequently stop her writing to look over the most recent finished pages, and each time she did such a review, she could not believe how few errors there were.

Sometime during the evening Mrs. Scrivener came in with a plate of food. "Thanks, Mom," she said, "I forgot all about eating. And also thanks for whatever story you've been giving Dad, because he's been in here only once trying to bug me into telling him what the big project is."

"It's okay for now Angie. But just get done, I can't manage running this interference for you much longer," Mrs. Scrivener told her daughter.

It was almost midnight when she came into the study again. Her voice showed annoyance when she spoke, "Angie, I insist that it's time you stopped working, and that you get to bed. I've been very tolerant until now, but its way past your bedtime, and I've been waiting to go to sleep myself. Your father has been sound asleep for hours."

"Yes ma'am, and now is a good stopping time for me. Mom, it's all written and in the computer. It just needs some final editing which I'll do tomorrow, and then it will be ready for printing."

The only words from Angie's mother in response were: "Thank GOD!" Then she marched out of the study and up the stairs to bed.

Angie gathered up her stuff and followed.

Sunday was a very good day for Angie. She was awake, showered and dressed long before her parents. She took a dish of cereal for herself and then went right to the study. She reviewed her story, did a computer word count which came out just right. She figured the pictures would not count as additional words, and she sure didn't want to go over the word limit this time.

Next there was a good tidying up of the room done including a gathering up of all the discarded hard copy. That she took up to her room until she could dispose of it in a secure manner. Finally, in her room with the trash, her completed manuscript with the photographs attached along with everything else she had worked with in the study, she decided to rest and relax for a few minutes.

Apparently the tension and anxieties of the last few days drained away when her big writing task was done. That was obviously so, because once she stretched out on her bed Angie fell fast asleep. She was dreaming about newspaper articles with various headlines on them and her name under each headline as the reporter who wrote the story. After several of those dream visions floated through her mind, the dreamer was hearing cheering and what she thought was applause. At that point in her reverie Angie awoke and after the few seconds it took to emerge from the dream world into reality, she realized that the clapping and the cheering during the last moments of her dream was a banging on the front door and the shouting of Benjee for someone to open it. Obviously, a parent had delivered him home from the sleepover and he didn't have a key. That meant that her parents must still be in their room.

That realization pushed Angie into action. If Benjee were home it was important that anything to do with her story be out of his possible sight until her submission was on the way to the HERALD. His nosiness she didn't need. In a flash she was at her desk. First she wrote the correct address on the large brown mailing envelope she found that morning on her father's study desk, and then she carefully slid in her completed manuscript and competition entry form. The photos that were selected to go with the story were protected by pieces of cardboard she scrounged from the back of a scratchpad. That she slipped in behind her manuscript. The envelope was securely sealed with transparent tape. It was put in the desk drawer with her notepad and the discarded printout pages. Deciding to take no chances, she even dumped into the drawer the contents of her wastebasket that contained the scraps of Mr. Jacobsen's note. She locked the desk drawer and pulled at it several times just to make sure the lock was holding fast.

Now she was ready to see what was happening with rest of the Scrivener family. Angie descended the stairs in a leisurely fashion with this thought in mind: *Anything Benjee does in the way of teasing or questions, I'll be cool and won't let him get my goat. I might even be a sweet sister.*

CHAPTER 7

▼

MONDAY

After what transpired in the Scrivener household since the previous Thursday, Monday morning began as a rather normal one. Everyone was together at the breakfast table. There was the usual bantering about who was going to be responsible for what chores during the week, allowances and lunch money was distributed. Benjee announced the days he would not get home by their regular dinner hour because there was an early deadline for the next edition of their school newspaper.

When breakfast was over Mr. Scrivener was the first to leave for his school. Benjee followed because he decided to ride his bike instead of waiting for the school bus. Angie was glad only she and her mother were able to have a few minutes together before her school bus would be at the corner. Angie went up to brush her teeth and put her backpack in order.

When she came down her mother was still at the table drinking her usual second cup of tea. Angie approached her and said, "Mom, you've been swell. I love you for that and everything."

"I love you too, Angie, but I don't think I can keep making up stories about what you have been up to until the HERALD contest judges announce their selection of the Plainview community Junior Reporter. Since I promised, I will keep trying. But I sure hope your father forgives me for all the white lies I've told him."

"Don't worry, Mom, when everyone learns that I'm the winner everything will be fine. In the meantime, my terrific mother, will you do me one more favor?" As she asked that question Angie pulled the mailing envelope from her backpack, handed it to her mother and said, "Could you go by the post office this morning and have them put on postage that will get a fast delivery?"

"Yes, Angie, but I'll do better than that. I must be in the city today on some hospital matters, and I'll make time to drop it off there. Will that be a fast enough delivery?"

"That's great, Mom. I repeat everything I said about love and a terrific mother. And Mom, I forgot to ask, did things work out about that transplant case?"

"Yes, dear, a heart was located, and I understand the man is doing quite well. Thank you for remembering."

"I'm glad," Angie told her mother as she swept up her backpack and was out the door to catch her bus. She was ready to face Nancy Omanski and her other classmates.

As she left Mrs. Scrivener quietly said to herself, "*I hope my daughter is* not *heading for a big disappointment. I don't know how we would all manage that.*"

Actually, school on Monday was rather uneventful. Angie realized that with her mind being on other things, she missed a lot of what the teacher was saying during class time on Friday. That plus the fact that she did not crack open a schoolbook for the whole weekend made it necessary to listen with complete concentration to what went on in class. What open time there was, she used for catch-up reading.

Whenever she thought there was an opportunity, Nancy tried different ways to get some hint from Angie about the story lead she promised. To stop the nagging of her friend Angie decided to take a small risk, so just before lunch period was over she said to Nancy, "If you'll stop bugging me for the rest of the day, I'll give you a hint."

"Sure, sure, give me the hint and you won't hear a peep from me for the rest of the day. That's a promise"

In almost a whisper Angie gave out her hint: "The big story you will soon be able to write is going to be all about me."

That piece of information did not exactly satisfy Nancy. It was the sort of news that just whetted her appetite for more details. She started to ask for more, but Angie cut her off with just a few words, "Nancy, may I remind you that among true friends a promise is sacred."

"Okay, you win," Nancy responded, "but I'm reminding you that my promise is for today only."

There was no further Nancy nagging, but off and on during the afternoon Angie wondered about how she would handle the situation for ten more days.

CHAPTER 8

▼

TUESDAY MORNING
AT SCHOOL

Tuesday morning something happened that was worrisome for Angie. She and Benjee were alone in the kitchen fixing their brown bag school lunches when her brother blurted out in his usual loud voice, "Hey, brat one, I heard you ask Mom last night if she dropped something off for you when she was in the city. Are you going to tell me about it?"

"Mind your own business," was all Angie said as she tried to make a fast exit from the kitchen.

Her escape was prevented when Benjee grabbed her wrist and pulled her back. "Oh no, little sister," he said as he tightened his grip, "you're not getting away with that kind of an answer. I picked up a rumor at the BANNER staff meeting about something big happening to you. How about it?"

Good fortune was again bestowed on Angie. Her savior mother came into the room in the nick of time. "Get your hands off your sister, go brush your teeth and get your stuff ready for school," she sharply commanded him.

"Yes ma'am, Captain Mother," and with that he let Angie loose, gave his mother a military-like salute and marched out of the kitchen.

"Another close one," Angie said, "thanks again, Mom.

"Yes it was, and I'm through keeping your brother away from all this secrecy. He senses something is going on, maybe it's time to place a little trust in him."

"I don't think that's the greatest idea I've heard lately," Angie responded, "but I'll think about it. So long, Mom, I'm off for school to chew out my supposed-to-be-friend, Nancy."

The first opportunity for Angie to speak with Nancy was not until the first period class session was over. There was a brief beak between math and social studies, and Angie cornered Nancy in the back of the room.

"You are avoiding me," she said, "you know you're guilty. You knew what I told you was not for circulation, but you couldn't wait to blab about it. You were the only source for my brother learning that I was involved in something important."

"I don't know what you are talking about," Nancy told her friend.

Angie was really beginning to show her anger. Forgetting where she was in a too loud voice she said, "You do so, stinker."

That remark of Angie's was a surprise to Nancy. Even though "stinker" was not so terrible, in all the time they were friends neither one ever called the other any kind of a bad name. Now it was Nancy's voice at a pitch not usually heard in a Plainview elementary school classroom: "Listen dork, friends don't call each other names like that."

Every eye in the class was now turned to the back of the room. Some in the class were gleeful thinking that a good fight might be brewing. At the same time Ms. Rivers rushed over and placed herself between the two girls.

"What is going on between you two…." but their teacher never finished her question because she was interrupted by an announcement coming over the intercom system. It was Mrs. Penner's voice saying, "Angie Inkster Scrivener, report to the principal's office immediately."

It suddenly became very quiet in the room. The announcement caught everybody when their attention was completely on the interesting developments at the back of their classroom. At first neither Ms. Rivers, Angie or Nancy moved from the positions they were in when Mrs. Penner's voice was first heard. It didn't take but a few seconds, though, for the teacher to regain her composure.

"Go to your seats class," she ordered. "Open your social studies book and reread today's assignment. There will be a quiz in a few minutes. That includes you, Nancy. Angie, get going to the principal's office. You heard Mrs.Penner. I'll deal with the two of you later."

Angie quickly left the room, but not without some concern. Starting her walk through the corridor toward the office she thought, *I'm in trouble. I forgot* to *bring a note from home about Friday's tardiness, and I bet Mrs. Penner told the principal about* the *story I gave her, and he thinks* it a *big fib.*"

When she approached the school office Mrs. Penner was standing in the office doorway waiting for her. Angie was immediately puzzled because she had a big smile on her face. She took Angie by the arm and gently ushered her into the principal's office. Now she was totally confused because his face was covered with a big smile, and his first words to her were, "Congratulations Miss Scrivener, you are going to be our school's heroine"

Such a pleasant and enthusiastic remark from Mr. Soberman was not what Angie was expecting, and for a few seconds she was speechless. Aware that both the principal and Mrs. Penner were still smiling and giving her warm looks, her usual capacity for talking returned. "Thank you," she said, "but please tell me what is going on here?"

"Yes, yes, of course," Mr. Soberman answered, "we shouldn't hold you in suspense. Not very long before you were paged, there was a call from the managing editor of the HERALD morning newspaper…"

When she heard that Angie felt weak in the knees and decided to hear the rest while she was sitting. Once in the chair she said, "It's okay, Mr. Soberman, I didn't expect that, I'm sorry to have interrupted you."

Mr. Soberman continued, "As I was saying, the man at the paper said that last night after deadline he was given the news story to read that you submitted for their Junior Reporter competition. He told me that it was news that should not wait to be printed until after the competition deadline no matter who the winner would be. They intend to publish it tomorrow morning as a story on the front page with your byline. What do you think of that?"

Angie's jaw dropped and her eyes opened as big as saucers. At first there was a pause with nothing being said, but then she exploded: "Wow! That's what I think. Wow, I don't believe it."

It was Mrs. Penner who spoke next, "Well, it is true. Tell her, Mr. Soberman, tell her the rest of it."

"The rest," she heard Mr. Soberman say, "is that at this very moment a team of reporters and photographers is on the way to your house to interview you and to take some pictures. A car sent by the HERALD should be here in a few moments to take you home. Hurry back to your room and get your things. Ms. Rivers has already been informed that you are to be released for the rest of the day. Again, congratulations."

"Wow again," Angie said, "but does my mother know about this?"

"She certainly does," was Mrs. Penner's answer. The person from the HERALD called your home first. Your father was also notified at his school so he'll be going home to be there for the picture taking."

Mr. Soberman added, "Yes, and messengers were sent to have your brother come down so he can also be there for the photo session."

Angie sort of winced on hearing that news, but her next question to Mr. Soberman perplexed him a bit. "Sir, may I please use your phone for a short call?"

Naturally, under the circumstances that permission was granted. Angie picked up the phone on the principal's desk and punched in a number. When the connection was made Mr. Soberman and Mrs. Penner heard her say, "Jacob, this is Angie. I have to talk fast so listen carefully. It won't be necessary to wait until next week. The story will be in the paper tomorrow morning. I think you better be ready to get THE JACOBSEN surfaced and up on the beach. I'll see you some time today."

No questions were asked about the unusual phone conversation, and Angie left to return to her classroom shrugging her shoulders as if she still didn't believe what was happening. Coming into the outer office she saw Benjee standing there with his backpack slung on his shoulder. He greeted her with the expected question, "Is it possible that you can now tell me what the heck is happening, and what kind of trouble we're in?"

Angie grabbed Benjee's hand and pumped his arm up and down while she said, "No trouble at all, brother dear. Meet the real newspaper person in the family. Mrs. Penner can tell you the beginning. Anything else you'll find out when we get home" With that she let his arm drop and she skipped through the door.

The walk back to her room was quite different than when she was on her way to Mr. Soberman's office. Now she felt as if she were floating on air like a puffy white cloud in the sky. Again, all eyes were upon her as she walked into class. Before approaching her desk to gather up her books and notebook she stopped at Nancy's place. In almost a whisper she said to her, "I'm sorry I lost my temper before—I guess we were both wrong. I'm going to ask Ms. Rivers if you can come home with me now. Your big story chance will start happening when we get there."

By this time Ms. Rivers pretty much knew what was going on, and she allowed Nancy to leave with Angie. It was plain to see that they were friends again, and that she could forget about what happened earlier in the rear of the room.

Angie, Benjee and Nancy sat in the back eat of the car sent by the **HERALD** for the drive to the Scrivener's house. On the way Angie extracted a promise from her brother. It was that Nancy was to have an exclusive for the BANNER on the story about everything that might take place during the rest of the day.

CHAPTER 9

▼

TUESDAY FORENOON AT
THE SCRIVENER'S HOUSE

As they turned into the Scrivener's street, it was obvious that all the neighbors who were at home at that hour were gathered in front of the Scrivener house. Parked in the driveway was a big station wagon with the identification on its door that read, MORNING HERALD ROVING NEWS CREW. Standing right at the main entrance door to the house there were two photographers with their camera gear at the ready. The driver of the car they were in honked to move people out of the way so he could pull up to the curb right in front of the house. He came around to hold open the door as the passengers emerged one by one.

Angie, Benjee and Nancy took a few steps toward the house when there was a shower of flash bulbs that went off and the constant clicking sound of pictures being taken. "Don't stop," the driver behind them said, "keep walking right into the house."

Once in the house the photographers followed behind them. Mr. and Mrs. Scrivener were standing at the foot of the stairs waiting for them. They embraced Angie and gave warm greetings to Benjee and

Nancy too. Angie managed to get her mouth near her mother's ear and told her, "No more white lies or crazy stories to cover me, Mom."

That was all she had a chance to say because Mr. Scrivener pulled her on the side to say, "Angie, I'm proud of you. You're going to be a good carrier of our family's tradition. And you were right to have kept what you were doing to yourself. That includes keeping your own father in the dark."

Aside from the photographers there were three other people now gathered in the living room. A man who appeared to be her father's age came over to Angie and introduced himself as Mr. Speliman, the HERALD's newsroom chief. He herded them into the living room in front of the sofa for a family picture. Benjee briefly lagged behind because he was giving Nancy, who was his paper's reporter, instructions about how to cover the story. Nancy found that her things along with Benjee and Angie's that were piled on the hall floor. She located her notebook and several pencils. Following her editor's instructions she managed to find the BANNER's camera buried in Benjee's stuff. From then on she snapped pictures whenever the HERALD photographers did and furiously made notes about everything she saw and heard.

When the picture taking was done, the newsroom chief introduced the two members of his reporting crew. The man was one of their veteran reporters who covered all the big stories for the paper, and the woman was the reporter who wrote their feature stories. They interviewed Angie posing question after question about her: investigation; Mr. Jacobsen; when she decided she wanted to be a newspaper reporter; her hobbies; and a host of other questions. Mr. and Mrs. Scrivener could not believe the poise Angie exhibited during the long grilling.

Even Benjee was impressed with her performance, and he was beginning to see his sister in a new light. As he watched and listened a lot of new thoughts passed through his mind: *I'll never be able to call her a brat again. She's acting like a true professional. Maybe I*

should stick to basketball and let her become the writer in the family. He couldn't believe what he was thinking, but that's the way it was.

The reporters signaled to their chief that they were finished with their interviewing. Mr. Speliman then asked Angie, "Ms. Inkster, do you know a way to get in touch with Jacob Jacobsen so we can interview him and get permission for us to personally get a detailed look at THE JACOBSEN?"

The man could hardly believe what Angie answered: "I already took care of that, sir. It's all arranged, and he's waiting for us."

"Young lady, you amaze me. You're a born newsperson. And that is a good cue to give you a letter our publisher asked me to deliver. I think, though, your family and friend would like to know what it says, so with your permission I'd like to read it."

Angie gave a gesture with her hand signaling that it was okay to read it. Mr. Speliman took an envelope from his inside jacket pocket, removed a fancy looking sheet of stationery and proceeded to read from it:

Dear Ms. Inkster:

I was very impressed with the high quality of the news story you submitted to us. Your writing talent is obvious, and the clever and methodical way you followed up on your hunches was a model of investigative journalism. The fact that it was done by such a young person marks it as a wonderful achievement.

Such work deserves to be recognized, and surely you are already beyond being just our Plainview Junior Reporter. I have, therefore, authorized our managing editor to offer you a position on our staff with the title of Junior Reporter-At-Large, This will give you the opportunity to report on events and activities of your choosing and submitting the stories to us for review and normal editing procedures. You will put in whatever hours you can so long as it does not interfere with your schoolwork.

Of course, you will be reimbursed at our regular rate for freelance journalists. I hope you will accept this offer. If you do, please schedule a conference with our managing editor. He will discuss all other arrangements and details with you.

Sincerely yours.
W.W. Walterson
Publisher. **MORNING HERALD**

There were gasps of surprise and mumblings of pleasure from everyone in the room. Someone started to applaud. Angie noticed that it was Benjee. She smiled at him and then blew him a kiss. The newspaper photographers missed that gesture, but Nancy got a good shot of it.

"I know you'll want to talk Mr. Walterson's offer over with your parents," the newsroom chief said to Angie, "but there is no rush about your having to say no or yes. Right now, I think you should take us to the spot where Mr. Jacobsen is waiting for us."

"Okay, but I know that my friend Jacob will not want a big crowd there. Only my family, my friend Nancy and you guys from the HERALD. I can see that there's an even bigger crowd outside than before. If some of them follow us, there is a certain point where they should be stopped. Can you make sure that will be done?"

Mr. Speliman explained that he was certain that could be done, but he would need to know where that should be. Angie told him they should be stopped at the end of Blossom Avenue before the entrance to the park and forest preserve. Mr. Speliman yanked a cell phone from his pocket and called the Chief of the Plainview Police. When he finished the conversation he announced, "Okay, the Chief needs about thirty minutes to shuffle some schedules, and then he will deploy a police escort to accompany us. They will meet our party here."

For the first time since the reporters began interviewing her daughter, Mrs. Scrivener spoke. "Look, people, it's surely lunchtime by now, and with all this excitement I'm certain everyone is at least a little hungry. It so happens that I thought this need might arise when I received the first call from the **HERALD** this morning, so I prepared some sandwiches. The wait for the police to arrive gives us time for them.

Help yourselves, you'll find them on the counter in the kitchen. And by the way, there are some conveniences I suspect many of you can use. There's one down here, and two upstairs. So feel free."

A chorus of "thank you, thank you" followed, and then there was something of a pandemonium. Everyone seemed to be talking at the same time, and there was a lot of rushing to the kitchen and the announced comfort facilities. Benjee made it to the kitchen first, and he came back holding a pile of half-size sandwiches. Now there was another surprise was in for Angie, Benjee wasn't digging into any of the sandwiches himself. He walked over to Angie and said, "Here Sis, take what you like. I think you need them more than I do."

Angie couldn't get over his behavior, but she did love the way he addressed her. She played it very cool saying, "Thank you brother, I think one will be enough for me. And, Benjee, I like Sis a lot better than brat." Benjee turned away quickly, found a place on the floor and began eating the sandwiches Angie did not take. Before he turned away from her, Angie saw that her own brother was blushing. That was another happening she could hardly believe.

Angie's Dad joined Angie on the couch. In a private way he said to her, "That was very nice letter from that W.W. Walterson. What do you think about his offer?"

"C'mon Dad, you know what I want. If you and Mom don't object, I'd like to accept." Mr. Scrivener smiled at his daughter, tenderly ran his fingers through her hair while saying, "Good girl, I knew you would make that choice. It's okay with me as long as your earnings don't exceed my salary." Without another word but with a big grin on his face, he wandered off toward the kitchen.

At that point, Angie was thinking whether she could still be alive while feeling that she had arrived in heaven. *Maybe heaven has come to earth just for* me, she wondered.

It was Nancy who heard them first. "I hear sirens. I bet that's the escort coming." Then she ran to a window for a look up the street, and practically screamed, "They're right up the block. Two motorcycles and a patrol car."

Benjee jumped up and scurried over next to her. "Nancy," he growled into her ear over the noise of the sirens, "remember, you're here as a reporter for the BANNER so stop acting like a banshee little kid."

Mr. Speliman told the photographers to gather their gear and pile into the station wagon and instructed the reporters to get in the wagon with them. He explained that he would drive the car that delivered the three young people from school, and that the person who drove them would take over the station wagon. It hadn't been Mr. and Mrs. Scrivener's intention to go on the next event, but Angie insisted that they should be in on the fun too. So they joined their two children and Nancy in the car with Mr. Speliman.

CHAPTER 10

▼

TUESDAY AFTERNOON
AT THE LAKE

The patrol car led the procession, Mr. Speliman drove behind it and the station wagon followed. One of the motorcycles stayed close to the procession on the left side with the other on the right side. Sometimes they would speed up ahead of the squad car to halt any traffic coming on the cross streets. All the while the police vehicles had their warning lights flashing and the sirens blasting. Sure enough there were a number of private automobiles trailing them, and at every block other cars joined the procession.

At the pace they were moving and no need to stop for any reason, it didn't take very long to get to the end of Blossom Avenue. There were already some policemen there who had set up a police barricade. The motorcycle patrolmen moved to the back of the HERALD station wagon to block any of the trailing vehicles from going any further. The patrol car pulled to the side, and the barricades were moved long enough for the Speliman car and the station wagon to get through, and then they were immediately moved to close off the park entrance road again. In a minute they were at the parking lot by the recreation building where the road ended.

The car stopped, and the station wagon pulled right next to them. Mr. Speliman turned to Angie and asked, "What's our next move? Give it to me fast because I need to call over to the other vehicle to let the crew know what they should do now."

"Tell your people to follow the stone walk to the middle of the beach and be ready for THE JACOBSEN's arrival."

Mr. Speliman called that instruction over to his crew. Immediately they all scrambled from the station wagon, and Mr. Speliman followed them. When they reached the beach Angie, her parents, her brother and Nancy were already there waiting for them. Angie took the short-cut path she knew so well through the wooded area that was a more direct route then the regular stone walkway.

If he was surprised at seeing them there, Mr. Speliman didn't say anything about it. Apparently he was now a little impatient about getting the rest of the story because he sort of barked at Angie when he asked, "So where is he? How does he know we're here?"

Angie knew THE JACOBSEN was just below the surface not too far out. As they were approaching the beach she saw the ripples in the water and a tiny piece of the Plexiglas dome, so she knew Jacob was waiting for her signal. "Watch," she said, "to the photographers and Nancy, and be ready with cameras." Then she made a beckoning motion with her arm, and almost immediately the Plexiglas dome moved well above the water level. A few seconds later the purple hull began to show, and soon the whole vehicle was floating toward them on the water's surface.

Benjee yelled, "Hey look, it's like a ship in the ocean."

"No, no, Benjee," Angie told him, "you wouldn't call it a ship, it's not that big. It's more like a small yacht even though it looks like a submarine. Of course, it is that too."

Everyone else was too fascinated by what they were seeing to say anything. When it was in shallow enough water for its automobile-like wheels to be seen, the newspaper photographers started snapping away. Nancy was just staring at it with her mouth wide open until Benjee yelled at her, "Take pictures, stupid, take pictures."

That jolted her from her trance, and she quickly joined in the picture taking. At the same time Angie announced, "Now's the big moment."

The scene now was just as Angie saw it on Thursday. THE JACOBSEN came to a halt in the shallow water, the clam doors in the front swung open, the telescopic metal arm lengthened until the claw on its end was hanging over the dry beach sand. It did the same job Angie knew it would do. THE JACOBSEN was pulled all the way onto the beach, the arm with the claw retracted back through the hull opening and the clam doors slammed shut. Using its own power, it then moved to a position right next to where the group was standing.

When it stopped the side door opened, the stairs came down and out scampered Jacob Jacobsen. He was in the same garments as when Angie first saw him, with his crazy helmet on and his control board hanging from his neck. Although Angie had described him in her news story for the competition and repeated those details during the session at her house, everyone still seemed surprised and a little uneasy at the sight of the bushy-bearded, wild-looking man. Angie obviously didn't think his appearance at all strange. She ran straight toward his waiting arms. Jacob scooped her up, and Angie gave him a hug and a smackeroo.

Despite their advance knowledge of what they might see, everyone except Angie seemed to be gawking as if what they were witnessing was not real. Mrs. Scrivener had her hand over her open mouth while her husband was holding her up with an arm around her waist. Mr. Scrivener realized that his wife's knees were buckling, and he thought she was about to faint. But she recovered when Mr. Jacobsen lowered Angie down to the ground.

It was Mr. Jacobsen who broke the ice and the silence with a warm greeting and a little speech: "Hello every one. I'm glad you could come. Welcome to the debut of THE JACOBSEN, the patent protected multipurpose vehicle that I invented and built. It's ready for commercial production as soon as someone comes up with the financing. Thanks to my young friend Angie Inkster Scrivener that may happen soon. Her courage, perseverance and news nose has stirred up the kind of publicity I couldn't do myself. For that matter, no public relations expert could have done it better—even if I could afford the cost of such an expert."

The rest of the afternoon was pretty much a repeat of what earlier happened at the Scrivener house. The reporters interviewed Mr. Jacobsen with most of their questions following the pattern of those they asked Angie. There were more technical questions about how THE JACOBSEN was built, what work tasks it could perform and others. Again, a lot of group and individual pictures were taken, and Nancy filled up all the blank pages in her notebook.

Although the interview with Mr. Jacobsen began while they were still standing around on the beach, after the early questions were answered, he then invited everyone to come on board. "As Angie can tell you," he told the group, "the control station module is quite comfortable. Tea, coffee and soft drinks are available, and there may be some other snacks too."

That invitation could not be refused so the questioning of Mr. Jacobsen continued on THE JACOBSEN. While the news crew was busy, Angie took her parents brother and Nancy on a tour of the vehicle. When the formal interview was over, Mr. Jacobsen showed off the details of his invention to the HERALD people. When everyone was assembled again in the control station module he issued another invitation. "How about a little spin both above and under the water?"

Before anyone else could respond Benjee was ready with an answer. "Yes," he said, "I thought you'd never ask."

Mr. Speliman was now worrying about deadlines for the first edition of Wednesday's HERALD, but he could see that his colleagues were anxious for that opportunity, and he knew that letting them experience the operation of the vehicle was an important aspect of the news story they were pursuing. Nancy was a little frightened of the idea, but she knew she couldn't let Angie know that. Mr. and Mrs. Scrivener were the most skeptical, but Angie urged them to do it.

After some hesitation, Angie's Mom did agree that they would go along. As she nodded her assent, she spoke to her husband, "Now what have our kids gotten us into? Will we be going through things like this for the rest of our lives?"

Mrs. Scrivener believed only her husband heard her questions, but quite a few in the group around her did hear them too. Those on board who overheard her chuckled a bit or smiled because of the seriousness with which she asked those questions. Benjee heard her, and he spoke up loud and clear: "You bet, Mom. That's the way it will be. There'll be one adventure after another for the Scriveners" That remark drew a good laugh from all the adults, but it was Jacob Jacobsen's laugh that was the longest and the heartiest.

They traveled a bit around the lake as a boat, but the view they got was only on the big wall screen. "The view is much better underneath," Mr. Jacobsen announced from his place at the control console, "we're going down."

Mrs. Scrivener grabbed her husband's arm and held tight. "We're sinking," Nancy screamed. She didn't want to do it, but she clung to Angie for security. Benjee plopped himself down in front of the big screen waiting to see the promised view. The sinking feeling everyone was experiencing passed away as soon as the craft settled down on the bottom of the lakebed.

Mr. Jacobsen was now away from the console and the main computer, and Angie knew from her previous time on board that he was through programming THE JACOBSEN for the events that were to follow. Sure enough, suddenly the front underwater light was beaming so brightly that the area in front of them was as bright as a sunny day in midsummer. What they were seeing, as Angie anticipated would be the case, was the one with which she was already familiar.

Everyone except Angie and Jacob were awe stricken at the beauty of what they were viewing on the wall screen. Nancy let go of Angie so she could move around to get a better view. The two photographers immediately trained their cameras on the screen to capture the unusual colors and images. Mrs. Scrivener walked over to Mr. Jacobsen and told him that just seeing the colors and the marvelous underwater life made her realize that she was glad her children did convince her to stay on board.

It was Mr. Speliman who broke the spell, "We must get back on shore," he told Mr. Jacobsen, "the pictures need to be developed and printed so we can select those we will use for press runs. These reporters must get their stories ready for the copy desk, and I'm supposed to be meeting with all the editors to make decisions on the makeup of tomorrow's paper."

It was Angie who spoke up rather than Mr. Jacobsen, "You don't have to worry, Mr. Speliman," she told him, "THE JACOBSEN was already programmed to surface at this time. Look at the screen; see how we are already above what you saw at eye level just a moment ago. Pretty soon the screen will show that we're above the surface of the lake."

From his place right in front of the wall screen Benjee looked back and asked her, "Sis, what's next?"

"Well, that was worth everything that's happened today," Mr. Scrivener whispered to his wife.

Angie smiled at Benjee. Then she said, "It's happening right now. Hear the whoosh of the vehicle's jets now propelling us toward the shore as a boat."

Jacob Jacobsen gave Angie an approving nod, and then turned to her parents, held up his hand with index finger and thumb formed in a circle. That was like saying to them, *"That's your daughter, and she is an okay kid."*

THE JACOBSEN'S climb onto the beach was executed perfectly. This time when the vehicle was on the shore Mr. Jacobsen instructed it to perform as an automobile. He sat at the console with his eye on the monitor as he keyed in the signals to drive his invention right up to the stone walk. When the exit stairs descended, they set down at the very edge of the walkway. The people that were passengers in the station wagon exited first and hurried to get on their way so deadlines would be met. The others huddled around Mr. Jacobsen at the bottom of the exit stairs as last minute details of who would go where and how were settled.

It was Nancy who noticed that the police had formed a patrol along the line where the woods met the upper end of the beach. The park and the protected forest preserve which comprised half the area around the lake was surrounded by a tall fence except at the main entrance gate. It was, however, possible for people to get to the beach area by walking through the woods from the other side of the lake. Since there were some who did just that, the patrol was keeping them back away from THE JACOBSEN.

"Well, that was to be expected," Mr. Jacobsen commented," but I think I should move out of here fast. There's no secrecy about this any-more, but I think I ought to have a more organized public showing and demonstration. Call me in a couple of days, Angie, when things calm down and we'll arrange it." He shook hands with Mr. Speliman and with Angie's parents. He bent over so Nancy could bang on his helmet to see how hard it was. He then spoke briefly with Benjee during which he promised him a private underwater cruise. To Angie he gave a thumbs up sign. She said to him, "So long Jacob, with an ɔ before the b, I'll see you later. Don't forget to buy a morning paper."

The strange looking, bushy-bearded inventor boarded his multipurpose vehicle, the stairs closed up into the hull as the hatch door came up with it and tightly sealed itself against the hull. As the vehicle moved away to get into the water, there was a round of applause and cheers from the onlookers being held back by the police at the rear of the beach.

While the farewells were being made, Mr. Speliman was busy talking on his cell phone. First he called his office to give instructions to hold all press runs until his return. With his second call he arranged for all the Scriveners and Nancy to be driven back to the Scrivener house with the sergeant who commanded the afternoon's police deployment. He would return to his newsroom by driving himself using the HERALD's car. The arrangements were that he would be escorted by one of the police motorcycles to hurry him through Plainview until they reached the highway into the city.

Mr. Speliman had a final request and some warnings before he rushed away. What he told and asked them was: "Listen, all of you, by this time the TV stations have surely gotten wind of this news event. I'm surprised their camera crews were not out here by now, but I'm sure they will be camped out at your doorstep. Would you do me a favor and hold off on telling them too much. Also don't let them get too much video footage. As much of this as possible ought to be a HERALD exclusive."

"Thanks for the warning, Speliman," Mr. Scrivener told him, "and don't worry about protecting your exclusive. I'll handle the TV situation."

As he was racing up the stone walkway to the parking lot, Angie called out to him, "Don't forget to tell your managing editor that I'm his new reporter."

CHAPTER 11

▼

THE END OF TUESDAY

The Plainview police patrol car with its siren blasting away and colored lights flashing turned into the Scrivener's street. True to Mr. Speliman's warning there were several TV crews. The video cameras were set up on tripods or hoisted up on the cameramen's shoulders. Angie recognized the reporter who was waiting with microphone in hand while some helper was behind brushing her hair. It was the anchorwoman from the evening news program when she first saw the video clip that gave her the idea for her news story.

As the police sergeant came around to open the rear door and lead them through the throng of news people and onlookers, Mr. Scrivener said, "Now remember the strategy we worked out on the drive here. We stay close together and follow the policeman up to our door. Don't be frightened by the bright camera lights that will shine on you, keep walking and ignore the questions that the reporter's will be shouting at us. I'll be the last one out, now go."

Every one did as they were told even though Mrs. Scrivener felt embarrassed about not being able to wave back to her good neighbor friends who were all trying to greet her in some way. When they were all in the house except Mr. Scrivener, he turned around in front of the doorway, held up his hands in a gesture to stop all the shouting. When he thought he could be heard, he began speaking, "Please folks, no statements and no more questions. It's been a long day for us, my daughter is very tired, and it is a school day tomorrow for the children. Perhaps tomorrow something can be arranged."

He paused briefly to shake hands with the sergeant and thank him for all the help he and his officers provided during the afternoon. Then he stepped through the doorway, slammed the door shut and turned the knob of the deadbolt lock. Once in the house, he turned to the others who were clustered behind him and said, "What a day! It was exciting, but I am glad its coming to a close."

Benjee's retort to his Dad's observation was somewhat different. He said, "It was fun, Pop. Let's do it again tomorrow." His Dad's glare told him that his father didn't think his remark was appropriate.

For a few moments everyone was either sprawled out on the floor or plopped down on the couch. It was a hectic day, and exhaustion was catching up with them. It was Mrs. Scrivener who broke the silence. "Nancy," she said, "I'm going to call your parents. I'm certain that by this time they know you've been with us, but we should relieve any concerns they might have. I'll tell them you ought to sleep here tonight. There's no sense in trying to run the gauntlet of news people still outside. They may not give up for several hours. You can borrow clothes from Angie, and I'll drive the three of you to school in the morning."

Nancy was enthusiastic about remaining at the Scriveners. Benjee wanted to call a friend of his to come over, but his Dad nixed that idea. Mrs. Scrivener slipped into the kitchen to call Mrs. Omanski.

"It's all settled," she announced when she returned to the living room, "but remember to call your folks sometime during the evening. Now it's time to get this household back to something that resembles normalcy. Arise, husband, so you can help me with fixing something to eat. Kids, you rest quietly, or do some studying."

For almost an hour normalcy did seem to prevail. There was salad and hot rolls with beverages served on trays in the living room. Angie, Nancy and Benjee bantered about one thing or another during the supper. Mr. Scrivener told tales about the imaginative, crazy excuses manufactured by some of his high school students to explain why they could not complete assignments. Compared to the unusual events and situations that marked the day until then, it was a rather relaxed and peaceful hour.

Suddenly there was chaos instead. Benjee jumped up dumping what was on his tray to the floor. "Hey," he shouted, "the TV, the news, it must be on already. Let's see if we made it."

He made for the stairway to get down to the TV in the family room. Angie and Nancy followed with Mr. Scrivener. Mrs. Scrivener didn't budge from her seat. Over the noise of pounding feet and the screaming of the two girls only her husband heard her say, "I'm staying here. All you're going to see is that awful scene when we looked so stupid with a police escort making sure we could get in our own house without being mobbed."

Mr. Scrivener did not remain with the children very long. He returned to the living room and said to his wife, "You're right, it wasn't a very nice picture. I was the most stupid looking one. That pose with my arms raised like they were was silly. It looked like I was acknowledging the cheers at a campaign rally. The kids are eating it up, that's for sure."

"That is exactly what I'm concerned about," Mrs. Scrivener remarked to her husband. "I am glad for the recognition and opportunity that has been given to Angie. You and I know she deserves it because she has the talent and the right ambitions, but I don't want her to get swell-headed from all this attention."

There was a lot of chatter among the three children after the TV evening news. Mr. Scrivener overheard them discussing how they should dress tomorrow for when they faced the TV cameras again. What he was hearing made him decide to put on his schoolteacher's hat and put an end to that kind of conversation. "Okay kids, I think the time has come to get back to reality. The three of you have already missed school and probably more tomorrow. So get up to your rooms, do some studying and then it's sleep time."

Actually there wasn't much studying done. The three young people were truly worn out from the day's events and were ready for bed not long after they were sent to their rooms. Benjee was obviously exhausted because he didn't even raise a fuss about being kept out of the bathroom for an extra long period.

Once under the covers Nancy and Angie conversed quietly for a few minutes. The last thing Angie said before she dropped off to sleep was, "Nancy, remember what I said about calling the police station and not telling the truth about who I was? Well, all the way back from the lake in the patrol car I was scared. I'm sure the Desk Sergeant I talked to on the phone was the officer who came with us. Am I ever thankful that he didn't recognize me. Nancy, that's another secret between us. Promise?"

Nancy didn't answer, and there was no secret for her to keep. She was sound asleep and never heard a word of Angie's confession.

▼

CHAPTER 12

WEDNESDAY MORNING

It was Mr. Scrivener who was up at the crack of dawn on Wednesday morning. Without awakening anyone he managed to get the car started and out of the garage. He drove first to the nearby supermarket that he knew on weekdays stayed open day and night. There he convinced the cashier to exchange a five-dollar bill for quarters. These he used at several newspaper vending machines he found in the vicinity to accumulate twenty copies of the HERALD.

After his last vending machine stop with all twenty HERALD copies stacked beside him on the front seat of the car, he picked one up to take a closer look at the front page. Until then he had only glanced at the headlines. He studied the front page for a moment or two, and then he spoke as if he were talking to someone sitting next to him: *"Whewee, this is more than I anticipated. The President of the United States could only wish for this kind of coverage. If this hits the national wire services our phone will be ringing off the hook. Every living member of the Inkster and Scrivener families in the U.S., Canada and wherever my father-in-law is at the moment will be calling us."*

When he arrived back at the house after his early morning shopping expedition, Mr. Scrivener found all the children and Mrs. Scrivener still in bed and sound asleep. He retreated to the kitchen; put the kettle up to boil; started the coffee maker; prepared all kinds of breakfast stuff and set the table. At each of the five place settings he put a neatly folded copy of one of the newspapers he purchased. When everything looked ready and to his satisfaction, he awakened all the sleepy heads.

It was a most appropriate coincidence when Mrs. Scrivener and the three children came into the kitchen at the same time. Mr. Scrivener was sitting at his place waiting for them. His greeting was: "Good morning family and frequent guest. I was up early so I did a little shopping."

At first no one caught on to what he was talking about, but then Angie noticed the folded newspapers. She practically dove for the copy at her usual table place exclaiming: "Oh God, I almost forgot about it. Thank you father."

Benjee, Nancy and even Mrs. Scrivener hurried to open their copies of the HERALD and get settled in their places. Soon everybody's eyes were glued to the first page. For a few seconds only the sound from the handling of the newspapers was heard, but then all kinds of exclamations were flying around: "Look at this!"; "There's my story!"; "The banner headline is two inches high; "Look at Mr. Jacobsen's beard!"; "Mom, Benjee's shirttails are sticking out!"

While the jumble of exclamations and comments seemed never-ending, Angie became the quietest of the five at the table. She was busy reading her story that was printed in a three-column spread on the right hand side of the front page below the full-page banner headline, which said:

PLAINVIEW SCHOOL GIRL SOLVES BIG MYSTERY

Over the three-column spread containing her story there was this heading:

HOW I SOLVED THE MYSTERY OF THE PURPLE AUTOMOBILE

BY

ANGIE INKSTER SCRIVENER

Angie knew, of course, that her story was going to be printed, but seeing it smack on the front page seemed like a miracle to her. There it was with her own name under the headline, and with her own face staring at her from an inset photo that was inserted in the story itself about half way down the page. It was exactly as she wrote it, except for a slight change in the headline and a few of her words that were deleted.

Looking up from her reading, Mrs. Scrivener noticed the glisten of tears forming in her daughter's eyes. "Ms. Reporter-At-Large, how does it look to you," She asked?

Angie had such a lump in her throat that she could hardly get the words out, but she finally said, "I think I'm going to die of happiness."

"I rather doubt that," said her mother, "and there is no need to hide the tears. Tears of joy are always welcome."

Two big round tears slid down Angie's flushed cheeks. Nancy heard Mrs. Scrivener's comment and turned from her reading to glance at Angie. When she saw Angie's tears, her eyes also turned watery. Mrs. Scrivener handed tissues to both of them.

Benjee in the meantime was examining the paper's front page with the eye of an editor. "That is some fancy page layout job," he observed. "I wish I had that many type faces to work with. And look how the three-column story on the right is balanced with the wide three-column one on the left. I like the head on that story—'**HERALD GETS**

SCRIVENER AND JACOBSEN TO TELL ALL'—The two reporters got large-type bylines too. Yeah, it's good, but if you ask me...."

It sounded as if Benjee was about to say that there were some edito-
rial improvements he could have suggested, but fortunately he was
interrupted by Nancy, "Hey guys, look, look what I found," she
shouted over Benjee's talking, "there's a special pullout section in the
middle of the paper. It's all in color with oodles of the staff photographers' pictures from yesterday. Angie, Angie, look, I'm in a bunch of
them. I've got to call home and see if my family has seen this yet."

As she went to the phone, Mrs. Scrivener called after her, "And
while you're at it, tell your mother I will call again just before we leave
the house. I would like her to meet us in the school parking lot so she
can give a hand in helping me with protecting you from the TV people. No doubt they're already camped out in front of the building."

Angie was pleased to see that some of the photos she took on the day
of her stakeout were included in the special section too. There was even
a credit line under her photos that said: "Photo by Angie Inkster Scrivener." She especially liked the one of Mr. Jacobsen in his funny outfit
striding toward her when he discovered her hiding in the woods. "I'm
glad I have the negative of this," she announced. "I'm going to have it
enlarged and framed as a gift for Jacob. He'll like that."

Mr. Scrivener suddenly jumped from his seat. "C'mon people." he
said, "it may seem like a holiday, but it isn't. If I don't meet my first
class, my principal will be giving me after-school detention. Excuse me,
but I must locate the school stuff I brought home yesterday which in
all the excitement I completely forgot about."

Mrs. Scrivener managed to get the three young people to put down
their copies of the HERALD and get ready for their drive to school.
Benjee objected, insisting that he could take care of himself and that all
his buddies would be on the bus waiting to hear his stories about yesterday. He was firmly convinced otherwise by his mother.

After snatching a few bites of food, the hurried call to Mrs. Omanski, and some hectic last minute preparations by everyone, they were ready to leave. Mr. Scrivener had a hard time finding some student papers he finally discovered were in his car. The result was that all the Scriveners and Nancy were ready at the same time. As they filed into the garage each of them except Mrs. Scrivener had several copies of the **HERALD** tucked under an arm. "Be cool, all of you," Mr. Scrivener called out as he backed out of the garage and was on his way.

Mrs. Scrivener drove off in her car with Angie, Nancy and Benjee. There was only one incident that occurred on the way. A few blocks from the house they passed the corner where a bunch of youngsters were waiting for the school bus. They saw who was in the car, and a big cheer went up. That wasn't too bad until Benjee rolled down his window, threw one of the copies of the HERALD at the crowd and hung out the window with his hands clasped above his head acknowledging their cheers. That caused an explosion. It was Mrs. Scrivener, obviously furious at Benjee's acting up. "Benjamin Scrivener, close that window and sit down," she yelled at him, "act your age. Don't be a show off. You know very well that the cheering is for your sister, not you."

There were some muffled giggles from the two girls in the back seat, but Benjee was so stunned he didn't say a word to them. He could not remember his mother ever yelling at him in that way, and it brought him to his senses very quickly. For a few seconds there was dead silence in the car, and then it was broken by Benjee's apology, "I'm sorry, Mom," he said very meekly, "you're right. That was stupid of me."

Mrs. Scrivener remained silent and kept her eyes glued on the road, but she did remove one hand off the steering wheel and gave Benjee a good nudge with her elbow. He knew that was a signal from her accepting his apology, and he slumped down in his seat with a sheepish grin on his face.

Angie leaned forward so she could whisper into her brother's ear. He heard her say, "I thought it was terrific. I know you did it for me."

Angie's whisper wasn't quite soft enough to escape her mother's ears. Mrs. Scrivener didn't say anything, but Angie's gesture brought a pleasant thought to her mind: *That's a hopeful sign; perhaps a new era has dawned for brother-sister relationships* **in** *the Scrivener family.*

When the turn was made at the next corner and the school came into view, there was a sudden burst of chatter in the car. Two police cars were standing at the entrance to the parking lot, and the area in front of the main entrance looked exactly like the Scrivener's driveway and front yard yesterday afternoon—the lights, the cameras, the reporters with their microphones ready and a throng of kids in back of all the equipment.

A policeman standing at the entrance to the parking lot was one of the officers who were from yesterday's deployment at the lake. He recognized Mrs. Scrivener at the wheel and waved them into the lot. There Mrs. Omanski was waiting for them with a comb and brush in her hand. She gave Nancy a hug and immediately began primping her daughter. A few words were exchanged between the two mothers, and then they were off to face the cameras and the shouted questions of the assembled reporters. Benjee walked in front with the officer who accompanied them. Behind them side by side between their mothers were the two girls.

By now all the busses had arrived so the whole school population was outside to watch the proceedings. As the procession led by Benjee and the officer came into view, the cameras started to roll and a chorus of cheers erupted. This time Benjee didn't respond. Remembering his mother's warning that it was all for his sister. He just kept marching forward keeping a serious look on his face. Angie looked from side to side as she waved to the crowd and shouted greetings to the familiar faces of kids from the fifth grade.

They were about halfway down the walk to the steps that led up to the main entrance when Nancy nudged Angie to get her attention.

"Angie, I think there's going to be some kind of ceremony," she said. "Look who is gathered on the stairs waiting for us. There's Mr. Soberman, Mrs. Penner, Mr. Story our English teacher, Ms. Rivers and a bunch of others I don't know."

Benjee overheard her and he looked over his shoulder and hissed at Nancy, "Some school newspaper reporter you are. Don't you recognize your own Mayor, and you should also know that the tall man next to her is Chairman of the Plainview School Board."

"I'm glad to see that you're alert to those things, Benjee," Mrs. Scrivener said to him as they kept walking, "and I see members of the Town Council are also up there."

Angie turned her eyes to the group gathered on the stairway just as a school maintenance man brought out the speaker's stand with the microphone and built-in loud speaker that was used in the auditorium when there were special programs.

"Now I understand," Mrs. Scrivener said to Nancy's mother, "that means there will be speeches by the dignitaries up there. That's the reason the reporters shouting questions at us like yesterday haven't hounded us. The TV people and the press have been instructed about a schedule that must be followed. Afterward, though, they'll flock all over us, and I want to avoid it. There's been more than enough media exposure for the kids already."

Nancy's Mom expressed some disappointment about how orderly it was so far. She expected to be stopped and interviewed about her daughter's part in yesterday's happenings, and that the two of them would have a special spot on the evening news.

By this point in their escorted walk, Mrs. Scrivener was somewhat more satisfied with the way things were going. In fact, she loosened up some, and she did a little of her own waving and nodding to familiar faces in the crowd. Benjee noticed the change in her behavior when he glanced back at her. "Hey Mom," he called back, "that's good. Dad told us to stay cool, but he didn't say we shouldn't enjoy. This is like a parade, it's great."

The parade did not last too long. The policeman and Benjee came within a few feet of the stairway when Mr. Soberman motioned for them to stop. The officer took Benjee under the arm and guided him off to the side. Mr. Soberman came down the stairs, spoke a few words to Mrs. Scrivener, and she briefly conversed with him. He patted Nancy on the head, greeted her mother, and then took Angie by the hand and led her up the stairs near the speaker's stand. Mrs. Scrivener motioned to Nancy and her Mom that they were to stand on the side during the ceremony.

It was not a long ceremony. Mr. Soberman spoke first and announced that school was officially canceled for the first period so all the students and teachers could remain outside for the program. He then made a little speech about how proud he was to be the principal of a school that could boast of a fifth grade heroine like Angie Inkster Scrivener. That brought a lot of applause and cheers. He introduced the Mayor who read an official proclamation. The main words in it declared that this day shall be known to all as **ANGIE INKSTER DAY.**

The Chairman of the School Board followed the Mayor. He announced that the Board met the previous evening to enact a special resolution. What he told the crowd was: "In honor of the wonderful publicity Ms. Scrivener's clever work and good writing brought to the Plainview school system, the resolution provides additional monies for immediate use by this school. This was done so a new computer system can be purchased for use by your school newspaper staff to improve the paper's appearance and to make its production more efficient."

The loudest cheer for that announcement was from Benjee, and he could be heard shouting, "That's my sister who did it for us." His Mom didn't reprimand him for that outburst.

Finally, after Mr. Soberman praised Mr. Story and Ms. Rivers for the great work they were doing with the fifth grade students, and he then asked Angie to say a few words. She nodded her head in agreement and mounted the box that was quickly placed there for her so she would be able to see over the speaker's stand. A hush came over the crowd, and then she began her remarks:

I know that my mother is worried that there is too much fuss being made over me, and about what I did. She doesn't want me to get swell headed, but I won't. A lot of it happened because I was lucky. Especially was I lucky to have helpful and understanding parents.

If Mr. Story hadn't made me stick to the rules for the fifth grade writing competition, I probably would not even have thought about entering the HERALD competition. And he always helped me with my writing.

Ms. Rivers taught me to keep an eye out for things going on around me and to be a good observer. And if she didn't step in between Nancy and me when we had that stupid fight, we might have hurt each other.

I thank Mrs. Penner for believing in me when I told her what my excuse was for being late to school last Friday. If she hadn't allowed me to use the phone when I made believe I was calling my Mom to tell her what happened, I'm positive everything would have fallen apart.

And to my best friend, Nancy, I thank her for helping to keep the secrecy I needed and getting some of my classmates to stop asking me questions. They were as bad some of the TV people yesterday.

Now I think I better get back to my schoolwork. If I don't catch up, I won't have time to search for more news worth using for a story that I can submit for my job with the HERALD.

Thank you, thank you everyone.

For a minute or so after Angie spoke her last words she just stood quietly staring out at the crowd. There were now roars of cheering and continuous loud hand clapping—her fifth grade classmates were really whooping it up. In the distance at the back edge of the crowd she saw a funny looking hat waving in the air. It was Jacob's crazy helmet with the antenna attached to it. She motioned for him to come on up, but he shook his head in a no sign. He blew a kiss in her direction as he turned to leave. Angie saw him go to his old truck parked up the street, but she knew that soon they would be getting together.

The ceremony was now coming to a close. Mr. Soberman called on Benjee and Nancy to come up onto the stairway to be introduced. Angie stepped down from behind the speaker's stand to meet them as they came up the stairs and were introduced. Then with Angie in the middle, Benjee on her right and Nancy on her left, they entwined arms around each other as they looked out at the crowd and acknowledged the cheers and the applause they were getting from their fellow students and all the assembled friends and guests. Their faces were beaming with joy.

After the applause and the hurrahs for them died down, Mr. Soberman declared that the program was over and reminded all the students not to be late for their second period classes.Mrs. Penner and Mr. Soberman quickly herded the three Scriveners into the principal's private office. Right after that Ms. Rivers and Mr. Story escorted Mrs. Omanski and Nancy into the office. That was the plan agreed upon by Mrs. Scrivener and the principal during their brief exchange of words before the ceremony began. That was the way for the children and the two parents not to be harassed until the TV crews finished their wrap-up feeds to their stations, and until all the reporters left to file their stories.

Second and third periods for the fifth grade that day were to be combined as a special class with both Ms. Rivers and Mr. Story in charge. That class was to have a little party and the opportunity to ask Angie and Nancy all the things they wanted to know about THE JACOBSEN, and there were a lot of such questions. They were interested in knowing if Nancy was scared during the underwater cruise, and there were all the sorts of other questions which children of their ages would naturally wish to ask of their own classmates who were part of an unusual adventure.

AS THE SCHOOLYARD CEREMONY DRAWS TO A CLOSE, NANCY, ANGIE, AND BENJEE FACE THE CHEERING CROWD

CHAPTER 13

▼

THE THREE DAYS
THAT FOLLOWED

Both at home and in school things pretty much returned to regular
routines and activities surprisingly sooner than expected. Mr. Scrivener
saw the Wednesday morning ceremony on the evening news that
night, and there was a nice story about it in Thursday morning's HER-
ALD. Mrs. Scrivener returned to her job at the hospital, Benjee was
busy with editing the next edition of the paper and writing his own
story as follow-up to what Nancy wrote.

Angie buckled down to her studies, but she skipped her dancing
class and a synagogue youth group meeting. By the end of the school
day on Friday she realized that the past week's activities and excitement
had exhausted her. She and Nancy talked things over some during
school hours, but there was none of their usual back and forth tele-
phoning. Angie was happy when Saturday came, and it was the quiet
kind of Sabbath that her family usually observed.

Early in the evening on Saturday she did go with Benjee and her
Dad for a visit to their grandmother. Mr. Scrivener's mother sometimes wasn't fully aware of things happening, but the helpers and

nurses did read to her from Wednesday morning's newspaper. She did understand that it was Angie making the speech on the television news. During the visit she was quite interested in the things Angie told her about the events of Tuesday and Wednesday.

Angie's investigation and stories about THE JACOBSEN did get on the wire services and make the national news. Just as Mr. Scrivener expected, the result was a flood of telephone calls from friends and family. Most came in the evenings and Mr. and Mrs. Scrivener handled them.

There was a special call early Friday morning from Mrs. Scrivener's father. He was supposed to be retired, but he still traveled all over the world giving lectures and doing consulting about new methods of book printing. He telephoned all the way from Moscow. Angie loved to talk when he called, and she was always anxious for him to visit. Unfortunately, this time she was in school at that hour, but he told Mrs. Scrivener to make Angie promise to write him all about her recent experiences.

On Sunday afternoon she had a lengthy phone conversation with Mr. Jacobsen. Right after that she sat down at her desk to write the promised letter to her maternal grandfather. This is what she wrote:

Dear Grandpa Inkster:

I wish you were not so far away so I could tell you in person about how interesting and exciting my life has been in the past days. I know that Mom has told you a lot on the phone, and Dad told me that he sent a fax to you with clippings from the big newspaper story. I'm sure you have it by now, so I won't go into all those details again.

It's sort of funny that I am writing you today because this morning's Sunday HERALD announced the winner of their Junior Reporter competition. A boy from our school in the sixth grade won it. That was the spot I was trying for before they made me their Junior Reporter-At-Large because of the story I wrote about the purple mys-

tery car. The Plainview school's Junior Reporter's appointment will only last until the end of the school year, and he will not get paid for his stories. I will continue as long as the stories I file will be accepted, and I will be paid as a free lancer (Dad says that is okay unless I make more than he does—hah!hah!)

I guess getting paid and stuff is not so important though. I know it's good to have this chance for it will help to make my dream come true of becoming a real journalist and someday maybe a famous TV interviewer.

Most of all I am glad that I am beginning to carry on the Inkster family tradition since I will be involved in something to do with printing and publishing. Of course, I'll be in the writing business too, so that should make the Scrivener side of the family happy.

My friend Nancy's story about the happenings came out in Friday's edition of our school newspaper. The headline on the story was, HOW I HELPED MY FRIEND ANGIE BECOME FAMOUS. Benjee edited the story and suggested that headline. It was a very funny story, and she is a good writer.

The best news is that I just heard from my new friend, the inventor of THE JACOBSEN. Jacob told me that in a few days there will be a big news conference where he will demonstrate all the practical work his multipurpose vehicle can do. He will also announce that a new factory will be built in Plainview to manufacture the vehicles for commercial sale. As a result of all the publicity a lot of investors have promised support. He said some of the models would carry the name "Angees". I think maybe he is kidding me. He is going to visit our school next week. He promised me he would wear regular clothes and have his beard trimmed. I'm sure he'll still wear his helmet. I think it is glued to his head. Oh yes, Benjee spent a whole night with him on his invention; they slept in the bunks while THE JACOBSEN was parked at that beautiful underwater place.

I have an idea for my next story for the paper. It is going to be about the nursing homes that take care of the grandmothers and grandfathers who need constant care. I learned from the place where Dad's mother lives that they need more volunteers to come visit residents who have no families in the area. The story will show what the volunteers do when they visit, and it will tell how even young kids can become volunteers.

Things seem almost like always in our house again. There is one thing that is different, and I know Mom and Dad hope it lasts. Benjee stopped calling me "brat", and he sort of treats me like a good friend. Also I don't feel jealous of him any more. Perhaps we've both suddenly matured—what do you think of that word for a fifth grader?

Please come soon and stay for a long visit.

Your loving granddaughter,
Angie

THE END
****

About The Author

Seymour Z. Mann received his Ph.D. degree from the University of Chicago in 1951. His interests were multi-disciplinary as evidenced by his having completed doctoral exams in Political Science, Social Psychology and Labor/Industrial Relations. Those interests were mirrored in the many facets of his professional career that have encompassed: teaching, research, and administration in University settings both here and abroad; practitioner experience as a labor union executive; serving as a consultant or advisor to an array of governmental agencies and non-profit organizations. All of these career involvements have provided a rich mix of experiences that he has drawn upon in pursuing the writing of poetry and stories that is the hallmark of his post-retirement years. Fuller biographical details can be found in any recent edition of Who's Who in America.

0-595-29907-5